Charlotte Carter is the author of an acclaimed mystery series featuring Nanette Hayes, a young black American jazz musician with a lust for life and a talent for crime solving. *Coq au Vin*, the second book in the series, has been optioned for the movies. Her short fiction has appeared in a number of American and British anthologies, including John Harvey's *Blue Lightning*. The first in a new series set in Chicago against the tumultuous backdrop of the 1960s will be published in late 2002 – early 2003. Charlotte Carter has lived in the American Midwest, North Africa and France. She currently resides in NYC with her husband.

**Also by Charlotte Carter and published by
Serpent's Tail**

Walking Bones

Charlotte Carter

Library of Congress Catalog Card Number: 2001048877

A complete catalogue record for this book can
be obtained from the British Library on request

First published in 2002 by Serpent's Tail, 4 Blackstock Mews,
London N4 2BT
website: *www.serpentstail.com*

Typeset in Bembo 12 on 14pt by Intype London Ltd
Printed by Mackays of Chatham, plc

10 9 8 7 6 5 4 3 2 1

Part 1

A.

A bit of history: She had come to New York to be a fashion model. History was on her side. For it was the moment in commerce when tall black women were sought after to stroll down runways. They also gazed smokily into the eyes of German cameras. They also stood with their backs to the photographer, legs apart, with leopard-spotted leather thongs vanishing up their ebony butts.

History had seemed to be on her side. Alas, she grew fat.

With stringent dieting and exercise she diminished, but not nearly enough. And there she was — a handsome and powerfully built woman of color standing nearly six feet tall. Irreversibly too big for the runway.

Her descent commenced. There was no job. There were silly jobs. There were jobs that deformed her feet: hostess, toastess, walker.

She moved into darker and darker neighborhoods.

And then, interviewing at a temp agency, she met a small gay black man, Rufe. For a time she lived with him in his small Greenwich Village apartment. He obtained less bone-shattering jobs for her. In time he obtained a small Village apartment for her. Nights, he took her into the bars.

The descent halted. She discovered in herself an entrepreneurial flair, first making oversize bags out of brocaded fabrics and then moving on to scarves and hats. Initially she sold them at street fairs and crafts shows and by word of mouth. The boutiques began to buy. She relocated to a loft in Chinatown.

She fell ill that November. But when the sickness had all run out of her, when the fever had long ago burned off and the terrifying cough was long gone, she was unwilling to leave her bed. Rufe, worried, knowing, but not putting a name to things, began dispatching messengers to the loft. In the green and white signature Balducci shopping bags: out-of-season fruits, butter biscuits from the north of France, fried chicken thighs. From the lesbian-owned independent bookstore: British *Vogue* and picture books of Rome and of Shaker furniture and fat biographies of Chanel and Vionet. When he phoned her, every day, Rufe said all she really needed was to get on her feet and get back to partying. Listen to your Aunt Rufe, he said over and over – that is how he referred to himself, as either Aunt Rufe or Uncle Pleasant—Listen to me. You just need a drink.

But Nettie refused. She remained in the loft with her fabrics and her TV.

She did recover. After Christmas, she was up, out, walking. And on the evening of January 8, 1998, she walked into the Rouge Lounge on lower Sixth Avenue to warm up after a therapeutic stroll.

She still answered to the name of Nettie Rogers. She was about six months short of her thirtieth birthday.

This was only her second time in the Rouge Lounge, but Nettie had decided she loved the bar. It did not partake of the hip. It did not ape the lower depths. It was not a pick-up bar. It was not an artists' bar. It was not a music bar. It was not a black bar. It was not a white bar.

She took the first stool at the front end of the place.

The bartender was a sweet roly-poly Frenchman. Or perhaps he was Belgian. She ordered a red wine and a glass of water. Nettie was wearing brown slacks, a long, loose gray fisherman's sweater under her lined raincoat, and a brown Basque beret. On the sound system, Dinah Washington was singing her pop R&B hits from the 1950s. Some were duets with Brook Benton.

The bar was full, but not jammed; no line of customers standing in a phalanx with their drinks behind the seated customers. The small tables on two sides of the bar, against the wall, were all taken. The dining room at the back was about half full.

It was seven o'clock. Monday evening.

She crossed her legs and sipped the wine. She lit a Kool Mild 100, took three quick puffs, and then let it sit in the ashtray.

For some reason Nettie had begun to think of her childhood friend, Louisa – probably because of the Kools, because they were the first cigarettes the two girls had tried, when they were eleven years old. Louisa had not finished high school, had not come east; she had stayed there. What would Louisa have thought of the Rouge Lounge? She would probably have just said 'Mercy' in that scathing, bitter way of hers.

Louisa was an ungainly girl. But the lecherous old men in that ugly, ungiving place where she and Nettie were born were after Louisa from the time she was eleven years old. Louisa liked them, too. And she would fuck for Chinese food. Sweet and sour anything.

Louisa taught Nettie how to sew. And it was to Louisa, and only to her, that Nettie had confided why she wanted to go to New York and become a model. She had no fancy justification for it. And it wasn't adolescent stardust. Simply the walk.

She wanted to walk, float down the runway, seen but not seeing, in gown after gown that caressed and consecrated her.

Louisa had said 'Mercy' to that too. But she had said it differently than usual.

Someone edged in beside her at the bar. On her right. Not touching, but close.

Nettie stared straight ahead, into the bar mirror on the wall.

Her neighbor, so to speak, was a white man of medium build, maybe forty-five. He wore a beautifully cut tweed suit and a muffler loose around his neck. His tieless shirt under the jacket was a deep dark luscious blue. Nettie kept her eyes forward – classic barroom etiquette in Manhattan. She got a good look.

His face was common enough, a bit Slavic and pugnacious. His eyes were cloudy but kind.

His only remarkable feature was his hair. Nettie was always fascinated by men's hair. His was sandy, long – much longer than that of the average businessman, which he gave every appearance of being – rough cut, and it seemed to spill every which way.

He ordered a Jack Daniels on the rocks. The drink came. She stopped looking at him in the mirror. She tried to think of Louisa again.

The man said:—I hope you don't mind my setting up shop here.

Nettie smiled. His voice was flat, well-bred.

—It's a free country in here, she replied.

—There was another spot down the bar. But I thought this place was the best.

Nettie said nothing.

—Do you know why? he persisted.

—No, I don't.

7

He leaned just a little towards her.—Because I have a thing for black cunt.

She picked up the water glass, wheeled on her stool, and smashed the glass against his cheekbone.

Blood leapt out, everywhere.

She ran out of the bar and did not stop running until she reached Fourteenth Street, where she leaned against the abandoned bank building and tried to button her raincoat over the blood-spattered fisherman's sweater.

B.

The staff of St. Luke's emergency unit sedated Albert Press and sewed thirty-one stitches in his face. Then he was bandaged, assisted into a wheel-chair, and wheeled to the waiting area. From his wallet they had obtained assurance that Press had a full-blown wraparound medical policy covering every conceivable blip in human existence. A private room in the west wing was prepared.

Albert sat erect in the chair, a bit vacant. The bandage covered his left eye completely, but he sensed that the eye itself was not damaged. There was no pain; simply a cymbal-like throbbing. Oddly, he felt fine. He dozed off.

A pressure on the top of his leg woke him. A woman in a striped apron and starched hat was by his side. She held a clipboard. Her voice was beautifully modulated.

—My name is Rae Tunick, Mr. Press. I'm with support services. Is there anything I can do for you? Someone you wish us to contact?

Press reflected the best he could on the question. His ex-wife lived in Philadelphia. She couldn't care less what did or did not happen to him. His father was still alive, but in a nursing home on Long Island and unable to differentiate between an apple and an orange; nor did he know his son's name.

There were his associates, of course, so many of them. After all, he had started, built, and sold two publishing companies. The first, an uncommonly prosperous law book company, that had anticipated the death of the fourth amendment and turned to publishing case books on racial discrimination and sexual harassment. The second, a press devoted to comprehensive, illustrated travel guides to major cities around the world. Books in the 'second time around' series approached travel from every conceivable angle: architecture, food and drink, gay guides, students-on-a-budget, splurges of a lifetime, and so on.

Always, he had made sure that his employees were taken care of financially and professionally. He had not signed off on the sale of his first company to the German giant, nor the second to the American trade-magazine conglomerate, until he had assurances in writing that there would be no lays-offs for eighteen months. He still consulted for both companies and every time he walked onto the premises he was greeted with genuine affection.

Yes, his associates would be shocked and concerned over what had happened to him. People in publishing always liked Albert Press. Because he was not pretentious. Because he was not oppressively literary. Because he had, over and over again, backed into success. He was not a financial whiz. In fact, he had little business acumen. He simply had the knack for dreaming up, or recycling, the right idea at the right time. A chance peg in a chance slot. The benefits to be reaped were bountiful. And now he had an awful lot of money.

I will give her the names of two business associates, he thought, but then he simply couldn't recall their names.

The kind woman from support services made a sudden move away from him, as though she feared being pulled under by his silence. Then she touched him sympathetically on the arm, and left.

The orderly loaded him onto the elevator and brought him to his room. There he helped Albert onto the bed, rigged up the night lights and buzzers, filled the water jug, and left. Press tried to sit up, couldn't, and flopped down – like a mackerel, he thought. Just before he fell asleep he remembered dimly a poem about a fish – it was a mackerel, wasn't it? Was it Marianne Moore? No, not her.

Detective Prego moved the chair carefully next to the bed of the sleeping man. He folded his arms, closed his eyes, and let his shoulders drop. It had been a long day. His face was red from the cold, his overcoat still buttoned.

Albert Press woke with a start an hour later.— Who? he asked, panicked.

—Detective Norman Prego, NYPD. Can you answer some questions?

—Yes. Of course.

Press spoke clearly, but out of the corner of his mouth, because the full facial bandage on one side inhibited jaw movement.

Prego placed a small recorder on the bed and flicked it on.

—Are you the Albert Press who resides at Amsterdam and Sixty-third Street?

—Yes.

—Do you own a co-op there?

—Yes.

—What is your profession?

—Publisher.

—Date and place of birth.

—August 4, 1958. New York City.

Prego leaned back:—Okay, Mr. Press. We got no good description from the bartender. We need your help on this. It was a woman, wasn't it?

—Yes. She was black.

—Light or dark complexion?

—I don't know. The bar was dark.

—But you knew she was black.

—Yes.

—Well, you know shades of black, Mr. Press. Right? Was she light-skinned? Tan? Was she pitch black? If you saw she was black, Mr. Press, you had to notice a shade. Just any shade.

—No, I don't know.

—Okay. What was she wearing?

—A hat. A brown beret, I think. A raincoat on the back of her chair. A gray man's sweater. She was a big woman. A tall woman. She smoked.

—Was she in the bar when you entered?

—Yes.

—Why did you go into the Rouge Lounge? Is it a regular stop for you?

—No. First time.

—You were in other bars? I mean, before the incident.

—Yes. Several.

—Do you drink heavily, Mr. Press?

—At night, yes. During the day, nothing.

—Were you inebriated when you entered the Rouge Lounge?

—No.

—How many drinks had you had?

—Maybe four, five.

—What were you drinking?

—Jack. On the rocks.

—Was your assailant inebriated?

—I don't think so.

—Well, take it from there.

—What do you mean?

—You're standing at the bar . . .

—Oh. Okay. She starts to talk to me.

—Were you surprised?

—No.

—Did you think she was coming on to you?

—No.

—What did she talk about?

—A movie she had seen. I don't remember the name. It was about a dying Englishman in Hong Kong, when it was reverting to Chinese rule. It stars Jeremy Irons.

—She talked about a movie.

—Yes, that's right.

—Then what?

—She told me she adored Jeremy Irons.

—Then what?

—I said I thought Irons was handsome, articulate, humane, insightful. But I just don't believe any role he creates.

—Then what?

—She struck me.

Prego thought to himself, This is bullshit.

C.

A bit of history. Rufe Beard was born in Jersey City in 1954, the son of Catholic Charismatics. The mother from the West Indies, father from Oakland, California. They both worked in dry-cleaning establishments. They died within a year of each other, when Rufe was sixteen.

At age fourteen Rufe was seduced by a former Jesuit who loved him; who taught him the vagaries of homosexual sex and imported gin, and who imbued the young man with a commitment to Situation Ethics: Always act in a manner that will increase the amount of love in the world.

Rufe joined the army and within one year was asked to resign, under the threat of Court Martial, for his sexual adventures.

Discharged from Fort Devins, Massachusetts, he journeyed to New York, where after a myriad of errors, many of them life-threatening, he established himself firmly.

Rufe waited calmly in the cold outside ABC Carpets, on Broadway and Nineteenth Street. It was ten-twenty in the morning. Nettie was already late.

Cock of the walk, he paced slowly in front of the store. Rufe was a fastidious and highly conservative dresser; but no matter how insistently his suit said Boston lawyer, his outrageous tie always spoke of New York arrogance.

He was little and fine-boned and dark-complexioned – much darker than Nettie. As a black man, he appeared so self-assured that he was often taken for a foreigner, usually an African. The self-confidence was no mere bravura. In fact, he had a true gift of gab and he was fearless and indubitably competent, a toy bulldog who had risen to the top at a temp agency – second in command to the woman who had founded the company – and was now in charge of corporate recruitment.

The job of course meant nothing to him except that it funded his life, which happened at night, played out in a serpentine pattern across Manhattan, from bar to bar, club to club.

It was only at night, in this mode, that Rufe resolved the contradictions.

And there were many.

For while putting love into the world was for Rufe a duty, a promise and a calling, he had also an infinite capacity for loathing. He loathed race, for one thing. Not his own; not that of anyone, really. It was the idea of race itself that he loathed, and denied, and dismissed. And class, and classes: Niggers, Whites, Women, the *haute bourgeoisie* and the *petite bourgeoisie*. All these, he despised. Yet, within each category he loved some and supported some and succored some.

He consulted his watch again. Ten-forty. Something had happened to Nettie. Their appointment had been firmed up. There was no mistake about that. Not that Nettie was so eager to accompany him. It was he who had the passion for furniture. But she, at least he hoped, had a passion for his passion – for wrought, turned, spun, painted wood. And she may have had a passion for his passion for fraudulent knockoffs of eighteenth-century tables; the ones that had the Rape of the Sabines and such enameled into the wood. Had he turned into another category he loathed? The aesthete?

At 10:45 he took a cab downtown to East Broadway. The bustling main street of the new Fukienese Chinatown. Nettie's loft building opened right onto the street, a sliver of a door between a tourist agency and a huge furniture store. The sidewalks were dense with people buying, selling, gawking, nodding. The street door was open as usual, as was the inside door to the stairs. Rufe marched through and up four flights of spotlessly clean stairs. He banged on the huge sliding door. He rapped ten, twenty times, until he discerned movement within. Finally the door slid open. She stood before him in an oversize raincoat.

—Honey, I was waiting, he said. Then he staggered backward, as if he had been pushed hard. He was struck dumb.

17

Yes, it was Nettie standing there before him. Maybe.

But maybe not. She had cropped her hair to the bone. It made her full face harsh, protruding, as if the wrong head sat on the body now.

She didn't say a word. She took his arm and pulled him into the loft, double locking the door behind them.

They moved through the living quarters with the cherry wood bed and the burled coffee table that he had given her, and the two sofas.

He tried a joke:—Spring cut? A bit early, isn't it?

Still silent, she maneuvered him into the work area with the benches and tables along the wall, the vintage Singer with its treadle, the bolts of fabric, and the finished bags and hats hanging on wall hooks.

She led him into the center of the space. The raincoat flapped open a bit and he could see that she was wearing a slip and nothing else beneath the garment. She was barefoot. Nettie's feet, slightly gnarled but always perfectly pedicured, had always thrilled him. In the summer, he always stared at them, smiling to himself.

She sat down cross-legged on the floor; seamlessly, fluid, like always. She made such movements easily – not quickly but easily – even though she was a large woman.

Now he noticed the things littering the floor. Not patterns or invoices or buttons and zippers and scraps from the hats and bags. It was actually scissored-up clothing.

Her brown Basque beret had been cut to shreds.

She pushed what was left of her old fisherman's sweater aside. He knew it well.

—What the fuck are you doing, Nettie? What's going on?

She didn't answer. She stared straight ahead and began to weep. She did not work up to the tears. They came instantaneously, in a flood.

Her suffering was unbearable. Rufe felt himself losing his balance.

He shouted at her, as if from down a long hallway:—What's the matter, girl?

Lost in the sobs, she made no answer.

If he had a gun, he realized, he would shoot himself, or her. Or both. He could not watch this.

—The beast, she said finally, snipping at the arm of the sweater.

—What?

She looked up at him. Stared at him as though he were the one not making sense.—The beast, she explained.

Rufe did not answer. She went back to cutting furiously. But now the tears had ceased.

—I've been waiting and I didn't even know it. And now it's here. It came for me. It'll get you too, Rufe.

—I won't let him get us, Nettie, he said, no idea what he was promising.

She smiled sardonically and shook her head.

But at least she had stopped crying.

She can cut up the whole fucking loft if she wants – at least she has stopped crying.

—Let me put some water up, he said.—Let's get some coffee.

He turned on his burnished high-heel brown leather boots, the tops hidden beneath the cuffs of his pants. As he walked toward the kitchen, the scissors indeed began to mimic the jaws of some sort of beast snapping.

A long night. Plenty of time for thoughts, fears, memories as she waited for sleep. Some went flying through her brain like dive-bombing mosquitoes. Others like tunneling worms, preying maggots.

Nettie got out of bed and searched for the long-handled broom. She rode it like a witch, ferreting out every scrap of fabric, every stray piece of paper, every dust ball in the loft. It was 2 A.M. and she was waxing the floor in her nightgown. She knew how crazy it was but she had to keep going until she wore herself out.

I'll wear you out, her mother had said. That meant she was in for a whipping.

Baby, I'm going to wear you out, one lover had told her.

Go to sleep now, you all wore out. A hand on her forehead. Whose? Nettie had had a kind of fit, that's all she remembered. Weeping until her lungs ached.

Louisa licking at an ice cream cone.—My mama say that's why niggers so lazy. Cause of how they used to treat us. Can you 'magine how they hit us with that whip? Work us like mules? And then they be all up on you if they think you pretty. If you pretty they don't send you into the fields. You don't get beat so hard. And the babies come out white but everybody know they not.

Can you 'magine?

Yes.

All the time.

Clumsy, dark, barefoot Louisa in one of those headwraps. Back bent, looking twenty years older than she is. Nettie, a wet nurse, a seamstress or a cook's helper or some other sort of house nigger, secretly passing extra fatback and cornbread to Louisa. Maybe Nettie has her own cabin. She'd call for Louisa as she lay writhing in raw agony, sweating, pushing out a mewling new life. And Louisa would know what to do. Sometimes in the daydream Nettie dies in childbirth. Sometimes there is a fine-looking colored man, a carpenter, who loves her; they dream of getting away but he is sold. No mother. No father. Sometimes the overseer finds her floating face down in the stream. Or, she gets hold of an ax, starts at the top floor, kills them all, the big house is running blood. And sometimes the master's son comes to her at night, a mendicant, and pours out his heart.

A rat in the kitchen. A worm in the brain. Nettie is almost worn out. She spills the dirty water down the toilet. God help me. Help me sleep. She draws a bubbling hot bath. By the time she is dried off and in clean night things, she is cold again, teeth chattering. But the sky is lightening. Sleep is here. And when she wakes, she will be in Chinatown.

D.

The room was quite bare except for a long industrial-type table. Two chairs with red plastic seats were on either side of the table. The overhead lights were powerful.

Detective Prego sat on one side of the table, Albert Press on the other. Prego's hands rested on a thick pile of strangely shaped papers, wider than they were long.

—Thanks for coming in, Mr. Press. How do you feel?

—Not bad.

Prego smiled.—I thought you didn't drink in the morning.

Albert laughed.—Did I say that?

—Yes. In the hospital room.

—A lot of pain in my face now.

Prego nodded. He didn't like what he saw. This man was almost out on his feet from booze. And he was dressed too light for the weather. Alkies did that, and the cold didn't touch them.

—Let me take a look, Albert said, running both hands through his sandy hair.

Prego hesitated. Could this man do anything in his condition? Could he identify his own prick? But he pushed the pile across the table.

—Okay, Mr. Press. What you see here is a computer selection of Afro-American and black Hispanic women between the ages of eighteen and forty. All are currently being sought on outstanding warrants. Take your time. It's worth a shot. The selection includes warrants issued under NYPD, state, and federal jurisdictions.

Albert nodded and pulled the warrants to him. There was a photo on each sheet, then basic biographical information such as date of birth, place of birth, physical description. Then a list of the criminal activity which triggered the warrant: aggravated assault, mail fraud, carjacking, credit-card fraud, extortion, robbery, possession and distribution of heroin, on and on. Then there was a note as to whether the lady in question should be considered armed and dangerous.

He found the first ten fascinating. The thought came to him that these warrants would make a wonderful anthology. A kind of grim coffee-table book. He could see it – the cover – perhaps a Herb Ritts. He could see the publicity on the book too – stark and mournful, but also exciting. Oh, it would have to be inclusive, white women as well. But it could be the ultimate post-feminist document. He started to laugh. He hadn't the slightest idea what post-feminist meant, but he liked the phrase.

Titles. He needed prospective titles for the book.

—What's the matter, Mr. Press?

—Nothing. Nothing.

His stomach, a burning pancake, flipped over. The Jack Daniels seemed to be laying on his larynx. He began to gag, but then conquered the filth rising in his throat. Titles. Yes, he needed titles. The Woman in the Window. Women on the Inside — no, Inside Women on the Inside. The Outlaw Is a Lady. Women on the Verge. Strongarm Sisters.

Oh, he liked that last one.

—You want to do this some other time, Mr. Press.

—No. No. Now. I can do it now.

Albert forgot about the anthology. He went back to shuffling the warrants.

Prego had settled into his chair. He was beginning to dislike this idiot. But then, noticing that a few drops of blood had seeped through the man's face bandage, he softened. This Press probably had to change the thing twice a day. The image of those shaky hands cutting, wrapping, handling blood-soaked gauze, made him cringe. Surely somebody else changed the dressings for him.

—Here! Look!

—What? Prego was on his feet, circling the table.—Did you find someone?

—Maybe . . . maybe this one, Albert said, tapping the warrant sheet.

Prego leaned over his shoulder. Norma Bessie. Thirty-four. Wanted for questioning in a robbery and double murder in a Queens Boulevard beauty parlor. Known to frequent drug locations in East Harlem.

—Are you sure, Mr. Press?

—No.

Now Albert was a bit confused. The shape of the face was the same. The physical stats were the same. This Bessie woman was big. The woman in the bar was big.

—A little too dark, Albert said.—And . . .

Prego interrupted angrily.—You told me in the hospital that you had no idea what the woman's complexion was.

—Did I? Well, I'm sorry. I think now she was light. He shook his head sadly.—No, this isn't the woman. Sorry. Sorry, Norma.

—Okay. Keep looking, Mr. Press. I'll get you some coffee.

Twenty minutes later Albert found another woman whom he identified as the assailant. Her name was Diane Stumps, a.k.a. Lucy Love, a check forger. Then he recanted. Ten minutes after Stumps, he came upon Laverne Moorehead. Twenty-six years old. Born in Camden, South Carolina. Last known residence: Brooklyn, New York. Small scar over right eye. Wanted on carjacking and weapons charges.

—Maybe this one, he muttered.—It just might be this one. He bent over the warrant sheet, his shoulders hunched. His face was close to the photo, very close. His lips almost grazing it.

Prego took a look.—No! Look, Mr. Press! You tossed out the other one because she was too dark. This one is coal black. So what are you telling me now? Your assailant wasn't light-complexioned?

Press sat up and stared at Laverne. No matter how he moved her warrant on the pile, he could not get her eyes to look at him.

—My feeling, Mr. Press, is that you ought to go home now and sleep it off. Come back tomorrow. You know what I'm saying, don't you? Sober and steady.

Albert Press didn't answer. The detective's words had offended him. Yes, he had had some unusual morning drinks. But no, he was not drunk now. Besides, this Prego was unsubtle. Cops often were. Prego was talking about a different kind of drunk. He was talking about a street alcoholic. They were ugly and dangerous. No doubt about that. But he, Albert, was different. With him, it wasn't only chemical. It was emotional, it was aesthetic. Stay drunk, Beaudelaire had said. Drinking was the whole world. It was hope. It was a place to go, a way to live.

Press had six bank accounts. And he had

enhanced the culture. But he needed Jack D. as much as Prego needed his badge and gun. Shame. No shame. People needed what they needed.

Albert shifted his chair a bit – and Laverne's eyes met his.

Prego was still talking. About booze and perception.

This one actually has terrible eyes, Press thought. Not like the woman at the bar. Hers were limpid.

Press smiled. What had his old secretary said to him: American capitalism has produced three cultural artifacts of note: Little Richard, Jack Daniels, and smart bombs.

Prego was now talking about a relative of his . . . a brother-in-law who had gone into a program at Smithers. Press wasn't listening anymore.

Albert Press, bent low over the table, whispered to Laverne Moorehead,—I won't turn you in. I'll never tell, because I have a thing –

And then he bolted upright.

A 'thing.' What thing? A thing for what? He was shaking his head, involuntarily. At that moment, Albert Press barely knew who he was. A thing for what? I don't know, I don't know. But he did know. At that moment he had the desperate, lunatic urge to cut away his tongue, or, better, to pry open his very head, reach in and snatch the words out of his mind – gather them in his fist and break them into pieces. But it would be like retrieving music.

The notes went out into the world and there was no taking them back.

He rose abruptly, irradiated, reeling. The words he had spoken to the woman in the bar were now the only words in the world. He remembered it all now. A thing for black cunt. That was a long, long way from a friendly barroom argument about the talents of a famous British actor.

—Are you okay, Mr. Press? Let's get some air. We need you healthy. That woman missed taking out your eye by a fraction of an inch. And the way I look at it, she was hell bent to put you six feet under. Go home, get fixed up, and get back here. These things always take time.

Time, Albert thought, is a skinny fellow in a steam bath.

E.

They left the noisy crowd behind and began to walk away from City Center: downtown.

He didn't speak for blocks and blocks. Not like him. He just cast those fugitive looks at her as they walked.

Finally he said,—You could've danced 'Revelations' better than that. You've got a ruffled parasol somewhere in the loft, don't you, honey?

Nettie laughed. But it wasn't her real laugh. She still hadn't got that back. And Rufe could still read the sorrow in her face.

He didn't speak again until they reached Thirty-fourth Street, with the last of the shoppers drifting around them. Then he said,—Is the nervous break-down over?

She said,—Is that what I'm having?

He said,—You didn't shave your head 'cause you want to be Grace Jones.

She cast her eyes down.—Rufe, you ever think of using one of those walking sticks? You're dapper enough to carry it off.

He said,—I'll take that attempt at humor as a sign

of recovery. Where are we going now—the Statue of Liberty? I mean, it's a bit late, but what the hell? In the last four days I've taken you to three museums, nine boutiques, one botanical garden, and an architectural walking tour of Chelsea. Isn't it about time you and I went into a fucking bar like civilized people and had a fucking drink?

They kept walking south. Three blocks later Nettie said,—Rufe, I can't go into a bar right now. I just can't do it, Rufe.

—Don't say 'can't.' Don't say you can't go. He raised a hand to silence her when she tried interrupting.—You're dealing with Aunt Rufe here, sugar. And who is he, a moron? No. He's a smart man. Now, the logical conclusion to be drawn from your behavior is that this nervous breakdown of yours, or whatever the hell it is, stems from an incident in a bar. How do you like those bananas?

At Twenty-first Street she stopped, put her arm around the little man.—Yes, all right. Something bad did happen to me in a bar. I don't want to talk about it, okay? Just let it lie. I cannot—

—Me, Nettie! You're dealing with me. Am I or am I not the last person in the world you have to hide an unfortunate drinking incident from? Who knows more about that shit than I do? Bad things happen to good people in barrooms. Even the great Rufe Beard has been eighty-sixed from a drinking establishment. It don't mean shit. You get back on the horse, Nettie.

—But you don't know, Rufe. This one you don't know about.

—I don't have to know. I don't want to know the particulars of your shame. Details? They mean jack to me. As you know, I detest soap operas. We're going to turn this corner, you hear me, girl, we're going to make a right turn right here and have us a drink at the first place we see.

He felt her weakening. As if her musculature were softening under his touch. He kept a guiding hand firmly at the small of her back.

The place, on West Sixteenth Street, was newly refurbished, and crowded. When Nettie froze in the doorway, attempting to turn back, he propelled her forward into the room.—That's what they do to the paratroopers, he said.—The ones that can't go, but they can't stay. The sergeant just pushes their ass out of the plane.

The rambling, comfortable room with its big horseshoe bar appeared to be a haven for the upscale youngsters who now worked and lived three to a room in the Flatiron district. But Rufe remembered when it resembled a turn-of-the-century saloon, the poor cousin to a *belle epoque* Parisian brasserie. The landmarks' conservation queens and interior designers used to love this place. The hamburgers had been marvelous. It made Rufe's heart sing to see the same bartender on duty.

There was only one free stool, and Rufe ushered her onto it. He ordered his martini immediately, and one for Nettie, with fruit. He got the bartender started on the next round as soon as the first one arrived. Nettie's drink had three olives crucified on a toothpick; trembling a bit, she plucked out the wooden stake and made quick work of them. In a minute, she took out her cigarettes.

An hour later, Nettie was grinning appreciatively at one of Rufe's famous shaggy-dog drinking stories.—What did I tell you? he crowed.—You still know how to ride that pony, don't you? Of course you do. You were taught by a master.

—Yeah, I'm on that pony now, she agreed, high, surrendering to it.—And I'm about to pee on him if I don't hit the little girls' room soon.

She slid off the seat and Rufe kissed her lightly on the cheek as she rushed by him.

There was at least one holdover from those days when the bar had been an 1890s-type saloon. They had kept the cut-crystal chandeliers running the length of the ceiling. Beautiful things to look up at. Nettie became even more unsteady on her feet when she returned her gaze to the far end of the bar, where a glowing sign spelled out RESTROOMS/ TELEPHONE. Seated alone right under the sign was an unassuming man she'd probably never look twice at. Except that one side of his face was covered by white gauze wrapping. The fear pounded at her chest like a chisel. She was standing in the dead center of the room now, and she knew that if she did not put one foot in front of the other, either walk forward or turn back, she would faint.

She saw the man hold up a finger, gesturing to the bartender. His drink arrived on the double and he placed a bill on the bar, next to what was already a healthy pile. Then he climbed off his seat and headed jerkily for the men's room.

She did not pretend even for a moment that the man she saw disappearing around that curve could possibly be any other than the one she had cut up in the Rouge Lounge. The man she had very nearly killed.

Nettie moved forward.

Albert was alone in the men's room. Nettie entered and closed the door silently behind her.

He was at the urinal, his back to her, shining hair spilling and curling like happy snakes around the collar of his fine jacket. He was weaving on his feet, head back, almost as if he were sleeping. He was zipping his pants now, turning to face her.

Nettie moved like a bandit — silent: Press's handkerchief whipped out of his breast pocket and tied around his eyes. His jacket pulled inside out and knotted, trapping his arms. When he was thoroughly imprisoned, she placed a thumb on his mouth and pushed at his teeth.—Keep your mouth shut, she hissed.

While she worked, he writhed and grunted in fear but he did not cry out. He was struggling to keep his footing.

Then, just when he seemed on the point of hollering, Nettie asked,—Ready for your thing now?

His pitiful thrashing stopped on a dime and he cocked his ears. A woman. It was a woman.

In one movement she undid his trousers and brutally extracted his member. There was an answering gasp from him. Then she smashed her handbag to the floor, spilling out its contents, and found her metal nail file. Nettie took it and pressed the hooked point harshly into his neck.

—Did you hear me? she said.—I asked if you're ready for your thing now.

He nodded.

Once more she grabbed his cock roughly.—You'd miss your thing if it was gone, wouldn't you?

A wheezy scream began to build in his throat then and she hushed it with pressure near his Adam's apple.

—I say, You'd miss your thing if it was gone. Isn't that right? But this time she did not wait for his answer.—Unless I misunderstood you? Unless maybe we're not talking about the same 'thing.'

His top lip twitched idiotically.

—Your thing is for a certain kind of cunt. Am I right about that?

That is when she heard the awful, unworldly sobs. No longer a strangulated expression of terror; simple, abject misery. She was flooded with shame and the tears rose in her own throat. Then she looked down at the man's penis, rock hard in her cupped hand.

—Oh Jesus, she moaned, and in the second it took to move her hand away, he ejaculated.

Nettie looked into his face then. The handkerchief was gone and he was staring directly into her eyes. Moreover, his arms were free. The Donegal tweed jacket was now soaking up urine in the glistening white bowl.

The man was now pressing his back into the tiled stall, hard enough, it seemed, to pass through the wall. He never stopped looking at her. And under his unblinking gaze, Nettie quietly gathered her wallet, appointment book, and makeup bag from the floor and stuffed them back into her purse.

—Ready for another one? asked Rufe.

—It's time to go, Nettie mumbled.—I rode the pony with you, Rufe, and it's time to go.

—That's right, he said,—but the next one is the charm. He pushed the martini gently into her hands.

Nettie extracted the olives and left them on the cocktail napkin. She turned the glass up and never took it away from her lips until it was drained dry.

—Go! Rufe said.

F.

Karen walked east on Fifteenth Street. By the time she hit Union Square her feet were aching.

The contracts were all signed now. She had sold the Fifteenth Street property, and the check that made it all irrevocable had been deposited via wire transaction to her bank in Rome.

Nothing else to do with the days, Karen covered the city, walking.

Lower Park Avenue was almost unrecognizable.

There had been no sweet little cafés or humming pasta restaurants in the neighborhood as she had known it. Let alone cell-phone boutiques, leg-waxing emporiums, dog-grooming salons. In fact, she did not recognize a single landmark other than the Guardian Life building at Seventeenth Street. That one was right off an old postcard.

Karen had been away from New York for nearly five years. She missed the city most in winter.

For the first two years at the job she had left the States for, she lived in Berne. Plenty of snow and azure skies, of course. But none of that wintry New York bustle. Sometimes the memory of Christmas in Manhattan would bring tears to her eyes. She yearned to be in the fray: Fifth Avenue, packed solid with people moving along like so many prosperous buffalo.

After two years, she was transferred to the Rome office. In casual conversations with strangers — invariably other Americans living abroad — she was always engaged in the old argument: which was lovelier, Paris or Rome? No contest, Karen always said. Rome. Though in truth she thought the debate was stupid.

She found a seat at the bar of a place that replicated a 1950s Parisian bistro. L'Express, it was called. The hotel where she was staying, the Gramercy Park, was only two blocks away.

Karen ordered a martini. She rarely drank them in Rome. Albert Press, himself a bourbon drinker, had taught her how to recognize a good one.

A bit of history: Someone had once told Karen that she looked like the actress Verna Bloom in *Medium Cool*. That, Karen recognized, was a round-about way of saying she looked like a hillbilly.

Which she was, more or less.

Most people up North drew very little distinction between whites from the South. Georgia . . . Mississippi . . . West Virginia. What did it matter? A cracker was a cracker. And that attitude seemed to go double for northern-born blacks.

Anyway, the Northerners were more right than wrong in the end; Karen had a lot to learn about the city, and she did look a great deal like the young Verna Bloom.

Karen never knew where her hunger for the New York publishing world had come from. She liked to read, surely, but had never harbored even the fantasy of becoming a writer. Finished at the community college, she had worked at the public library by day and waitressed by night, just long enough to save up the air fare and a few months' living money.

She took a typing job and a small, terrible apartment on Fifteenth Street near Tenth Avenue. A dark nowhere block in those days. Not far from the highway; not far enough from the roopy old sex hotels and gay porn houses along West Street. This was no place for her to be living when the time came for her sister to visit from Rock Hill.

But Karen was a quick study. Before long she was walking the New York way: bold, quick, and directed. Soon the fearlessness in her stride was genuine. She now exchanged greetings with the same neighborhood hobos who had once struck fear in her heart. They called her Honey and she called them each by name when she treated them to coffee or handed over spare change.

One job followed another and little by little her drawl fell away, as if her words had been pared with nail clippers. Now it took quite a few minutes before people asked—Are you from the South? and when they were told yes, clearly they were charmed rather than suspicious.

At home one Sunday morning in March, she spotted an ad in the *Times* Help Wanted pages. Wanted: editors for a new series of guidebooks. Decidedly offbeat ones. They were looking for people with wide knowledge of six specified U.S. cities.

Karen prepared a resumé calling on the creative writing energy she had apparently been suppressing all her life. She as much as claimed the title of world's foremost authority on greater Miami.

It did not take the managing editor long to decide against her.

But the owner of the company, Albert Press, had insisted she be given a chance. A firm believer in the hands-on style, Press had sifted through the job applications alongside the editor. He also knew her resumé was bogus, but he admired the applicant's temerity. Besides that, he pointed out, they had never had a Southerner on the staff.

And so, bypassing the usual process, Karen was interviewed and hired by the publisher himself. After the Christmas party, she and Press began an affair.

His generosity was almost unbelievable. When the landlord co-oped the building, Press lent Karen the money to purchase the Fifteenth Street apartment and the two equally decrepit ones that flanked it. As the housing market grew tighter and gentrification swept steadily west, she had a valuable asset in the huge and lovely apartment her old hovel had become.

Unlike most newly divorced men, Albert never talked about his marriage or his ex-wife. Whenever Karen invited him to do so, he would merely say that the fault was all on his side. He harbored no bitterness but just wished to move on.

The affair was not a particularly volatile thing. Albert Press was the kindest, the least volatile person she had ever known. Still, there were long stretches of time when the two of them were apart. Invariably, it was Albert who initiated the breakup. Actually they were not so much breakups as lacunae, as Karen took to calling them. It was a word Press had taught her. Albert would periodically back away from her, declining to discuss his reasons and declining intimacy – both in the nicest possible way.

Some of the interruptions in their relationship were caused by his month-long drinking bouts when he sealed himself off from everyone. And then there were the ones prompted by his involvements with other women.

A year and a half before Karen accepted the job that would take her out of New York, a friend told her that Press was seeing a 'stunning young black woman,' Faith, who was fast rising in the publishing world. Things seemed very serious between Press and the beautiful Faith, her friend said. The two happy lovers were being seen together at all kinds of industry functions; in the toney watering holes, heads turned. Karen waited, expecting to hear any day that Albert had married. But a few months later she learned that Faith had vanished. Quit her high-paid position without notice, moved away from the city. Suddenly gone. And not with Albert.

It was a Saturday morning when he phoned Karen again. He asked if it would be all right for him to drop by with croissants and salmon. They had not seen one another for months and so they spoke of many things during the long afternoon, but he made no mention of Faith. Karen determined that she would keep silent on the matter as well. But curiosity got the better of her and in bed that night she blurted out the question—Did you love Faith?

—Yes.

—And so?

Again, all his fault, he conceded. And really, there was nothing more to be said.

It was so strange that at this distance – five years – Karen could not recall whether she and Albert were on or off at the time she was offered the job in Berne. Karen had tried to explain it to the same friend who had kept track of Press's affair with Faith: nothing else had ever motivated her to leave Albert, nothing except this once-in-a-lifetime job offer.

—You've been shamed into leaving that asshole, her friend supplied.—Thank God you're getting free of him.

Karen had a good life in Rome. And she still loved Albert Press.

In the past three days she had phoned his westside apartment too many times to count. No answer and no answering machine. Not very likely he had given up drinking. She couldn't help imagining him face down on the pavement, in the alleyway behind the kind of handsome restaurant where he used to take her for lunch.

Finally, last night, she had staked out his apartment building. When it got to be ten o'clock and he still had not appeared, she crossed over and began to interrogate the doorman as to Press's whereabouts. The slim young man in uniform, a Hispanic, could or would tell her nothing, even when she offered money. Karen pushed past him and threw her weight on the superintendent's bell.

An older white man emerged from the ground-floor apartment. Karen gave him a minute to get a good look at her. She spoke softly to him. It would not do to appear like a wronged lover out for Albert's blood. At last the super remembered her.

Oh yes, he told her, Mr. Press still lives in the building. But he's staying temporarily at a hotel — in Soho. For business reasons.

Part 2

G.

Rufe was sharp that morning; gray suit, black silk shirt, blacker tie.

He sat behind his desk and stared out the window across Fortieth Street. He could see nothing but the building across the street. It was 11 A.M. His next business appointment was at 2 P.M., way downtown.

The walls of the office were bare. He believed in bare walls. The desk was clear of everything except the phone, a yellow legal pad, and two Mont Blanc pens: one ballpoint and one roller ball, one with black ink, the other one blue.

He began one of his self-happy interior monologues, a habit he had gotten into as a very young man to screw up his courage.

—What a dapper motherfucker you are, Rufe. So neat, so *au courant*, so absolutely charming. You are shit turned to sugar. You are God's little black martini. You could tapdance into heaven sucking Richard Gere's cock.

He ended the monologue, leaped out of the chair, did a little tap step, then a one-two boxing combination against an imaginary opponent, then sat back down, lay his head on the desk and said:—Jesus, punch my ticket.

Where will we go tonight? Rufe began to doodle on the pad: circles, triangles, little faces.

At 11:30 there was a knock at the door and Claire, the receptionist, stuck her round face in.— You have a visitor.

—Of the masculine or feminine persuasion?

—A man.

—Business or pleasure?

—He looks like business.

—Then by all means show the gentleman into the maw. We have temps. Little temps. Big temps. Depraved temps. Angelic temps. Harlequin temps . . .

Claire shut the door. Rufe quieted and folded himself into position, Nero about to toss a grape to the hermaphrodite flutist. He had over the years developed a certain technique for meeting people, a certain style. The first impression he gave was that of a stone faggot; then the faggot vanished completely and he turned into a shark. It was a very effective maneuver.

But the moment this visitor walked in, the usual mask fell away.

The bandage on the man's face was just too dis-concerting. No one had ever walked into his office before with a face like that.

It's Igor, Rufe thought – Igor, the drooling, limping, half-human lab assistant from a thousand old creature features. Igor, in Brooks Brothers. And look at the briefcase. Bottega V. – or Rufe was a monkey's uncle.

Wall Street? No, not financial services, Rufe thought, his shoes were too scruffy. Maybe a non-profit, with an independent income. He had that mop of *über*-Kennedy hair, too much for a man his age.

—My name is Albert Press.

Rufe did not offer to shake hands.

—What type of business are you in, Mr. Press?

—I'm retired.

Rufe laughed.—Our people don't do house cleaning. You've come to the wrong agency.

Albert Press put his case on his lap. The movement somehow unnerved Rufe. He didn't like the man or his manners. He pointed at Press's bandage.

—An altercation?

—An accident. I'm not here for temp services.

—Then what can I do for you, Mr. Press?

—You were in a bar two nights ago.

That threw Rufe, for a moment.—I'm in a lot of bars. Every night.

—In the West Village.

—I'm in the West Village every night.

—The name of the bar is Trio's. You were there until around eleven. You were served by a bartender named Harold. Red-headed.

—So?

—You were with a woman. A light-complexioned black woman. You came into the bar with her.

—So?

—I found out your name and where you work from that bartender. I want to find out her name and where she works from you.

—Now, do you?

Press did not pick up on the sarcasm.—Yes. It would be most appreciated.

—Appreciated? I get it, my friend. You saw a pretty yellow Ne-grooo gal across a crowded room. You were attracted to her. You want to meet her. You are deeply enamored of her. My my my, this is one of those life-affirming moments. Mr. Press, may I ask you something?

—Of course.

—What do you think of my mode of dress?

Press actually looked appraisingly at Rufe before answering.—Well, I think you dress quite nicely. Stylish.

—Thank you. And my speech?

—I would say that you are an educated man.

—You really think so? That's strange. Because there must be something about me that leads you inexorably to the conclusion that I am a pimp. What a silly error. Do yourself a favor and get the fuck out of here before I have to read you right.

The moment Rufe spoke the words, he regretted them. The man seemed to disintegrate in front of him.

Press began to mumble.

—What? What are you saying? Rufe demanded.

—I understand. I understand.

Then Press got up, laid his case on Rufe's desk, opened it and took out a packet wrapped in tissue paper.

—Would it be too much to ask to make sure that woman receives this?

Rufe didn't answer. He stared down at the package. He stared at Albert Press. The visitor walked out.

Rufe waited just long enough, then carefully parted the tissue.

Inside was a beautiful light blue beret — Nettie's style, but not her color — adorned with a tiny silver horse.

And there was a small sealed envelope — obviously a note of some sort.

How banal. Rather sweet in fact. But the whole thing profoundly agitated Rufe, for no reason that he could understand. He locked the hat and note securely in his desk and left the office.

Rufe strutted downtown in the cold, window-shopping all the way. His two o'clock appointment was on Murray Street. He had plenty of time. He was tense, very tense. The muscles of his neck hurt. He had that tight feeling in his ass, and his shirt collar was rasping against his neck.

At Twenty-first Street and Eighth Avenue he ducked into Crescendo.

The manager was behind the bar. He looked up, startled.—Never thought I'd see the prince of darkness in daylight.

Rufe's mode of behavior in bars was constant witty chatter with bartender and patrons. But now he said nothing but—Is it daylight?

The manager made the drink – Beefeater martini, straight up, extra dry, no fruit.

Rufe drank it very quickly and dawdled over a second one. The manager picked up on his mood and left him alone. It was a young bar, soft rap on the sound system, interspersed with disco nostalgia.

The problem, he realized, was not the gift for Nettie, nor the fool who had brought it. They both seemed harmless.

What really was bothering him was his own response to that fool – his I'm No Pimp schtik.

The fact was, he knew full well when he first met Nettie, even before he started hanging with her, well before he grew to love her, that she was in very bad shape. Much worse than now, but in a different way. Then, she had truly been out of it. She was wandering the world as a model *manquée* – a zombie – an insane mixture of narcissism and pathological shyness.

So he had started taking her on his rounds, and slowly she had become alive, human.

And as she was emerging, he had in essence pimped for her.

Oh, not for money. Or for perversity's sake. But

simply because he knew she had to get into the swim, and that meant sex. She had to start reacting to events. And fucking was the ultimate animating event, wasn't it? Every bit as vital as alcohol. As daring and tragic as murder. First there had to be the act. The fact of the act. Plain, funky, raucous fucking. Only afterward do you get into the hearts and flowers and the hundred-dollar scents. Only after you've done it do you begin to philosophize.

He had procured men for her in subtle ways. He had introduced her to men he thought she might like. Of course, most of them she did not like. But they were men who knew what to do and knew what they were doing. The affairs came and then they went. And Nettie was alive.

Why, Rufe thought, didn't I simply tell Press that I used to pimp for Nettie, but Iceberg Slim rescinded my member's card a few years ago.

Why did I let that silly white man force me into a pathetic defense of myself? Into that high-handed fakery. I may be a posturer, but I am a posturer by choice, Goddammit.

Rufe suddenly burst out laughing. He always mocked race. It was a bubble, a boil, a bunion, or a bauble. To treat it as anything else was just plain stupid.

Nettie put the package on a worktable in her loft. The heating system had malfunctioned and she was wearing three sweaters.

Rufe had left the message on the machine that someone wanted her to have a gift. Then he had it messengered to her in a stapled-up shopping bag.

She ripped open the top of the bag. A gift? Who wanted her to have this gift? Who else but Rufe himself would be sending her stuff anyway?

She turned the bag over and spilled out the contents. The light was dim in the loft that afternoon. At first she thought it was a large piece of fruit or a head of lettuce.

The little silver pin caught her eye first. Then she ran her hand along the top of the beret. Fine wool. From Scotland.

Suddenly she brought her hand to her mouth, as if to stifle a scream. There was no scream, but she knew exactly who the gift was from.

She placed the beret on her head. It was a bit too large. She walked to the mirror and studied herself, then returned to the table, removed the hat, and opened the envelope.

The note was written in an almost childish script, very close to printing.

—I apologize – if you'll pardon the cliché – from the bottom of my heart for what I said to you in the Rouge Lounge, and for not recognizing you in Trey's. I know from both incidents I have caused you great suffering and probably derangement. My own suffering and derangement are fully deserved. I wish to meet you and end this. Do you know what I mean?

And then there was the name, address, and phone number of Albert Press.

In a sense it was a relic, a playbill. She had cut his face to shreds in one bar. She had jerked him off in another bar. He was her beast. She was apparently his. So, finally, each of the beasts had a name.

Nettie said the name aloud – thrice.

She sat for a time in the low light, exhausted.

I wish to meet you, he wrote. Meet! What – have a coffee somewhere? Or a drink, more likely. Like normal people. As insane as it sounded, logic dictated this path. And self-preservation. He knew her first name now, knew Rufe, and knew that Rufe and she were friends. If he transmitted that information to the police they would find her and she would be in a great deal of difficulty.

Mr. Albert Press was right. It was time to end it. She would contact him, forgive him, thank him, whatever, and end it.

A few icy particles hit the window. Like the sky was just too tired to snow in earnest.

She made herself an omelet and two pieces of toast. Then she found herself unable to eat it. Instead, she ate the remains of a chocolate bar from way back in the refrigerator.

It's dreary now, she thought, all over the world. She began to gather the magazines strewn over her work area. Nettie thought of her magazine consumption as 'watching', not reading them, as if they were television. Sometimes she absorbed the words and sometimes not. Always she absorbed the pictures of the girls caught in mid-stride, the hems of their dresses bouncing, flowing, swishing, trailing behind them like ocelots. She could feel the silks on her back. She could feel her thighs straining against the jerseys. She could feel the eyes on her – the eyes were a kind of garment too – as she danced down the runway in those heels with the gossamer ankle straps. And the eyes found not a single imperfection no matter how hard they looked. And no sooner than they could blink, she'd be back again, in a different outfit, walking just as serenely as the last time. An illusionist.

She piled the magazines neatly on a table edge and then went to call Albert Press.

The phone rang only once. He picked up as if he had been waiting only for that call.

—Yes?

—Hello.

She heard him catch his breath.

—It's you? he asked.

—Yes, it's me.

—Would an hour be too soon?

—No.

—There's a comfortable cappuccino place on Twelfth Street, just west of Broadway.

All she said was:—Fine. She pressed down on the

button to disconnect, but hung onto the receiver for a while before replacing it in its cradle.

Nettie put the beret on again and at once her spine straightened severely. She walked across the loft, arms swinging loosely, chest forward, her eyes in their sockets blank as marbles.

She was startled to see her reflection in the hall mirror. As she began to apply her lipstick, she heard Louisa's mocking laugh, everywhere.

What are you doing these days, Louisa? . . . Is that a fact? Mercy! . . . Me? Oh, I'm a model.

H.

It's closer to six than to seven, Simon thought. He never wore a watch.

The tall, thin, dusky man in a blue overcoat was standing in the dank evening on the corner of West Tenth and Waverly. He was against the building line, staring across the street at the bar called Jimmy's.

He had taken the subway into Manhattan from Queens where he lived and worked, something he rarely did anymore, to meet his old friend Rufe.

But he was supposed to meet Rufe at Joe's, two blocks away, not at Jimmy's. Rufe wouldn't be caught dead in Jimmy's.

Simon laughed out loud, a bit derisively. He wanted no part of Jimmy's either. Not now.

Ten years ago, however, or was it fifteen, Simon Padilla was just another hustler in and around that skanky fag pick-up joint.

He was young, beautiful then, an exotic – from South America. Actually, Simon Padilla was born and raised in the Bronx.

He had somehow survived the plague. Why or how he could never understand. Whenever he did come into Manhattan now, on no matter what business, he found himself taking this pilgrimage.

Why him, and not the others?

So many gone. Everyone he knew was dead.

Now, he wasn't even gay anymore. He was just alive and celibate. He made his living by illustrating nature guides: *The Birds of Mexico, Mushrooms of the Eastern United States, Whales and Dolphins of the World, A Field Guide to Deciduous Trees, Wild Flowers of the Southwest Desert*, and the like.

Between jobs he traveled on money left to him by a dead lover. It didn't matter where he went or how he got there or how long he stayed. He just went and looked and walked and returned – Paris, North Africa, the Shenandoah Valley, Nepal, Namibia, Paraguay, Iceland. He traveled.

Why had Rufe called him after all this time? Maybe the little fellow was lonely. Maybe one of the night crowd he ran with had dumped him. Maybe he was sick of buying strangers drinks. And after all, he, Simon, had been one of the great pub crawlers and back-room bunnies, in his day. Prince of the bath house. But that was then.

Why had he accepted Rufe's invitation? That, Simon couldn't figure out either. Except, maybe, one always missed Rufe. In the way one missed the tumult in the next apartment after the battling neighbors moved out.

He peered hard into the scene, from a distance, through Jimmy's large and smoky window. The scene was the same. The men at the bar, old. The hustlers, young. But they were no longer the pretty fifteen-year-old golden boys from Surf World . . . and he didn't see those wiggy, handsome, bone-thin colored boys with roped muscles and spotlessly clean running shoes. The young boys inside Jimmy's now were from someplace else. Crackheads, by the looks of most of them. When it was good and dark, of course, the chauffeured limos would begin to arrive. The genuinely rich old guys getting sucked in the backseat and in return sucking the youth out of some borderline retard from the Plains.

Okay. Pilgrimage complete, Simon thought. He spent the next half hour or so in a bar off Sheridan Square. He had a black coffee and a brandy.

At five minutes before seven, he ambled in to Joe's. This, he realized, must be the restaurant's fifth incarnation. It was not and never had been a gay bar. As a rule Rufe didn't go into gay bars unless he was cruising. Gay bars, he always said, lacked tension.

His eyes swept all along the bar. He spotted Rufe in the center of the bar, standing next to his seat; Rufe rarely actually sat on his barstool. But surely he wasn't drinking alone. Where was Nettie? Not there. Or was Simon just having trouble recognizing her too? No. Nobody who looked even remotely like Nettie.

Maybe it was her day off, he thought.

Rufe was compulsively generous. Always ready to supply his friends with drinks, cash, a sympathetic ear, and sage advice. But for the friend, it often felt like work to be the recipient of that largesse.

Rufe insisted, for example, on choosing your signature drink. The one that best expressed you. The one the bartender in his favorite haunts would know you by. (—The closet case at the end of the bar is a J&B man if ever there was one. Let us send the poor creature a drink by way of the barkeep. But for you, Simon Peter, something Italian – with fizzy insouciance. You shall drink Campari.)

Rufe was your savior when you couldn't make the rent. But you had to accept Rufe's terms for the loan – namely, you would not be allowed to repay him, ever.

You had to listen appreciatively to his verbal high-wire act. No matter how drunk he was. No matter how drunk or tired you were.

You had to concede that the plan of action he devised for solving your problem was the only rational one.

And there was something else: You had to sparkle, be gorgeous, as Simon had been, as Nettie had been. Throw off the light of your beauty for Rufe to bask in. You had to be good bait. Attracting the eye of any and all interesting people. The pretty boys. The real men. The hungry, adventuresome couples and the wealthy dykes. And the brilliant old professors with stinking breath. Anybody with potential. Rufe was forever talking about the potential of strangers.

Simon was trying to remember Nettie's last name. It wouldn't come to him. After all the hours they'd logged drinking together, it was weird that he couldn't recall her last name. He had not seen her in . . . it must be close to two years now.

—This is my friend Nettie. She is a mannequin.

So went Rufe's introduction the first time Simon and Nettie met.

—Pardon me, he had added.—I meant, former mannequin.

Nettie was full and ripe with a kind of South Sea Island look. A beauty, yes. But far too big to be a model. Simon took her for a drunk. He assumed that was what accounted for the vague, passive quality in her manner. She couldn't be stupid. Rufe would never take up with a stupid girl. He might adopt a beautiful, dull-witted boy. But not a woman.

Simon and Nettie came to like each other but never developed a friendship separate from Rufe. Rufe always seemed to know what she was thinking. Simon never did.

Rufe, the Fixer, had hooked Nettie up with quite a few men. Simon couldn't understand why a woman as good looking as Nettie needed Rufe's help. After all, hadn't she once moved around in the swift world of fashion? The designers were fags, true enough, but what about the predatory photographers and all the powerful het men who lived to exploit pretty women? He even asked Rufe if she was a virgin.

—For all practical purposes I guess she is, Rufe answered.—One suspects there may have been some Midwestern goatherd with bunions, back home. Mayhaps a Pullman porter.

Rufe had just as tirelessly applied himself to vetting and getting boyfriends for Simon. Short-term or long-term. Old and young. For profit or pleasure. According to Simon's needs. And then there was the equally important task of weeding out the unsuitable candidates.

This place was getting crowded. Old Rufe was holding court as usual, in the thick of a conversation with two people, probably strangers, playing with the stack of money piled up on the bar, his money, ready for all in need.

Simon started toward him, then stopped. He felt queasy, unsure. That was Rufe, wasn't it?

He continued to look at Rufe from a distance. Six months probably since he had last seen him. Something in Rufe had changed.

Or had it? That was the problem, Simon realized. He wasn't looking at Rufe the way he used to look at him.

He wasn't looking any more at Rufe the wit . . . the cynic . . . the stylish little outlaw . . . the desperado of the Beefeater martini . . . the arbiter of what is cool . . . the gay conscience in the straight world . . . the master debunker / fly in the ointment in the gay world.

Depression swamped Simon, like a wave. He wanted to lie down. All he saw now was a preening little man – James Brown as Fauntleroy.

I.

She arrived fifteen minutes late. The moment she walked through the door she saw him at a table, his hands folded on top of it. She sat down across from him. His facial bandage was spotlessly white. He seemed thinner to her. She seemed smaller to him.

It was as if the chieftains of two feuding desert clans had decided to meet, to make a truce before the feud wiped out all living members of the tribes. They would swallow their hatred, exchange a few pleasantries, divide up the turf and part. Each one had to avoid making errors of speech because each considered the other profoundly unstable.

A moment after she sat down he pointed to the wall behind the counter, where the menu was presented on a chalkboard.

—What would you like?

—An espresso.

He called out the order to the young man behind the counter.

Within the studied calm of each, the eyes of each were nervous.

Her coffee arrived.

He said to her,—I am forty-one years old, then proceeded to tell her where he lived, his work history, his marital history.

The presentation was brief and precise.

He stopped talking abruptly. She realized he was waiting for her to return the conversational volley.

She told him her full name, where she was born, where she lived, and how she made a living.

Then she sipped her espresso. She was not frightened about being across the table from him now, or apprehensive, or guilty, or angry. She truly felt calm, appropriate. Only one strange feeling intruded and that was the sense that the world knew why they two were there together, which it clearly did not.

—It was a madness, he said.

—Yes, it was.

—I began it, I instigated it, I brought you into it. What a dreadful creature I am, Nettie. You may find this difficult to accept, but what brought me to your side in the Rouge Lounge was simply the fact that when I saw you I thought you were the most beautiful woman I had ever seen drinking in a bar in New York. And all I wanted to do was bask in your presence. He laughed self-deprecatingly.—Like a basking shark. Is that a species or a behavior? He stirred his coffee.—I had been drinking. I was not drunk. He smiled, bitterly, wretchedly.—The words grabbed me, Nettie. Do you know what I mean? By the throat. Would you prefer I call you Miss Rogers? Sometimes I have the very strange feeling that words and feelings are entities, out there, like a virus, just floating about, ready to hook their DNA up to yours. And in bad weather the phrases don't want to get wet, so they seek out any port in the storm. Am I making any sense?

She didn't answer. She was staring at his bandaged face. It was almost impossible to believe, right then, that she had actually done that damage. But she did have the feeling that she would like to look beneath the bandage, to see just how and where the cutting had been done: how deep, how jagged, how high, how close to the eye, how many stitches.

As for that incident at Trio's . . . she could not tie this man to that event, though it had to have been him she had mugged, in a way, terrified, humiliated.

—So, he said, suddenly less morose,—it was a madness and we're done with it. A plague of locusts that came through, ate the leaves, spoiled the trees, and then were off.

—Yes. The madness is over, said Nettie.

—You cut your hair, he noted, breaking into her thoughts about locusts.

—Yes, I did. Before the madness was over.

—Did you like the beret I sent?

—The fabric is lovely.

—And the pin?

—I like horses.

—I bought two berets for you, and two pins.

—Two? That seems—

—Excessive. I know. Well, not really. But it did seem excessive to send them both at the same time.

She wanted to laugh, but somehow could not, yet.

—I have the other, still. Since the madness is behind us now, since there is no longer any . . . any thread of it left . . . and we can be . . . just people . . . I mean, may I give it to you? I don't have it with me, but I'll be downtown tomorrow around three P.M. Not far from you. Near the South Street Seaport. Can you meet me there? For a moment? Near that big moored sailboat – the Peking Clipper. It would take only a moment, and I really want you to have it. And we are over all that now, aren't we?

She hesitated and he filled in the awkward silence in a rush:—Well, I can messenger it over if you wish.

—I can meet you. As you say, for a moment.

They drank their coffee in silence and then left after shaking hands. The odd thing about it, Nettie thought, is that as I am walking away from him, at this moment, I have already forgotten the way the man looks and dresses.

The only thing that remained with her was his thick sandy hair, and the white bandage, of course. He was a piece of fabric mounted on a pole and flying in the breeze. She burst out laughing. I am, as he said, beautiful, but not in the way he meant.

J.

Ever since the plane delivered her from Rock Hill via Atlanta, Karen had thought of herself as a New Yorker. Maybe even before that.

Not anymore.

There seemed to be grand new places to live, shop, eat and drink around every corner.

The strange thing was, Manhattan now seemed more like a European city.

To begin with, there appeared to be hundreds and hundreds of Europeans about. But it wasn't just that.

It was more civil now. More welcoming. Cleaner. And, in a kind of mimicry of the great dead cities, geared to the tourist trade. Every neighborhood in Manhattan had taken on a quality of virtual reality. Yes, that was it. To the adventuresome visitor, Tribeca and the East Village were the counterparts to the hill towns and rugged coastal villages of France, Spain, Italy, where the intention was to convince the tourist that life had changed little since medieval times. A kind of bait and switch.

Albert was staying in a plush new hotel in Soho. It was absurd. But so like him.

Maybe, just maybe, she conceded, there was some rational excuse for it. But one thing was clear: the building superintendent's vague explanation – business reasons – was not to be taken at face value.

No, that was some tale Press would have mumbled as he slipped the man a hundred-dollar bill and instructed him to collect the mail until further notice.

It did not take long to find him. There were only three hotels in Soho and the adjacent neighborhoods, and one of those was the Chinatown Holiday Inn. Not even for a second did she think that Press might be there. Except, perhaps, if he was planning suicide.

Albert had once said if things ever came to that point, he would either take a plane to the south of France and check into a château he knew about, high above Saint Tropez; consume a wonderful meal and a spectacular bottle of wine, then go back to his suite and splatter his brains all over the monogrammed pillowslip. Or, he would check into the local Holiday Inn, swallow a bottle of pills like a sissy, and then, wearing silk pajamas purchased specially for the occasion, ease into bed with a volume of Dickens and die thinking about Pip.

Albert was registered at the Granada, a luxe building near the foot of West Broadway where two bored-looking black men in Armani casual wear stood outside the revolving doors smoking. Both looked more like assistant managers at a trendy day spa than hotel doormen.

Mr. Press was not in at the moment, said the fellow at the desk. Did Karen want to leave a message?

No.

There was a café directly across from the hotel that looked as if it didn't do a great deal of business. She went in there. Karen sat quietly at a front table as the white sun struck at the frosted window like a laser. The bartender was steaming milk for her hot chocolate.

—What would you do if I said I was going to have a child, Albert?

Summer had arrived early that year. Only May, but the night was muggy. She and Albert were drinking margueritas at an outside table.

—But you are very diligent about contraception, he replied.

—Yes, I know, she said, patient.—I just meant if.

—I don't know. I guess I'm no good at imagining things, he said. Pause.—But surely a child would interfere with your work?

She smiled.—Good point, Albert.

—It isn't abuse, Karen assured her friend, who described Karen's relationship with Press as something out of a Fannie Hurst novel. The friend was forever encouraging Karen to look out more for herself.

—Really, it isn't abuse, she insisted.—Albert's wonderful. He would never hurt me knowingly.

All true.

Plainly, however, it had never occurred to Press to ask her to marry him.

—Do you like Erroll Garner? he had asked that first evening.

—I'm not sure, Karen answered.—Who is he?

Even though he laughed, she knew he wasn't really laughing at her.

His was exactly the kind of apartment she thought a glamorous New York publisher would have. The furnishings were modern, but the view of the night-time skyline from the high-rise windows was the same one in the typical art deco fantasy the Hollywood studios fed the public in the early 1930s.

She watched as he hunted incompetently through a pile of cassettes. In a minute, the brandied notes from that man's piano were rolling off the walls.

—'Misty', Albert said.—You're old enough to know that one, aren't you?

Press had had a great deal to drink at the Christmas party. When he joined her at the window and slipped one arm around her waist, she could scent the liquor on his breath.

—Shall I get you something to eat, Karen? We could order it.

—No, thank you.

—What about a drink?

—Oh no.

He kissed her mouth tentatively. They began to dance a bit.

—Will you stay and make love with me tonight? That would make me happy.

—All right, said Karen.

—I hope I'm not offending you. I mean, we've never even gone out to dinner.

—No. I would like it too.

Karen had not slept with many men before. Even so, she judged him as slightly awkward in bed. The sex was regulational the first time and with only a few exceptions, continued that way throughout the years.

One evening she and Albert were sharing Chinese food at his apartment, travel brochures, annual reports, and spreadsheets littering the big dining table. On impulse he asked her to accompany him on a business trip to Jamaica.

Her first sight of the white beach was thrilling. Karen could not wait to get into her new Diane von Furstenburg two-piece.

Albert was gone for most of the day. Meeting with the authors of the book he planned to publish. Interviewing freelance photographers. And, as he put it,—talking to people from the bank.

Typical vague Albert-speak. What bank? Talking about what?

She asked him if he had some kind of investments down here on the island.

—Yes, in a way, he said.

She went shopping with the fat cash allowance he had given her. She swam in the diamond-bright bay, signed up for aerobics in the hotel pool, indulged in a massage, wrote postcards to her sister, had her hair done.

When Albert returned to the hotel at night, they dressed and went out for grand, lingering meals at which he consumed astonishing amounts of liquor.

Two nights before they were scheduled to leave, he raped her.

He had had a particularly arduous day doing business, he said. Things had not gone at all well. He came back to the room looking distraught. Usually Karen was the first person he confided in about his business affairs. Not this time. He was in a brooding, agitated depression.

They ordered dinner from room service. Albert ate nothing, drank heavily. When she was done with her food, he went over to his briefcase and extracted from it a jewelry case. He presented her with a double rope of exquisite black pearls.

Overcome, she put them around her neck and swirled around the room. He barely glanced at her.

—Take your clothes off.

The harsh command brought her up short. A far cry from his customary cooing invitation—Come and lie close to me, Karen dear.

74

—Albert?

He walked up close to her. One hand on her breast, the other undoing his pants.

—Hurry up, he warned.

Before she could manage to undo her skirt, he had pulled her down onto the carpet.

He used his belt to lash her across the buttocks and back several times. Karen knew immediately the blows were not in the spirit of play.

She let out a startled yelp when he snatched her up and used the belt to bind her wrists together.

Albert tore at her underthings and used his mouth upon her as an instrument of violence. And then took her as if he planned to eat her flesh afterwards.

She lay under him weeping. And coming. Loving him, helpless and knowing it.

Albert slept for many hours. He came to in the early afternoon of the following day. Karen returned from her mud pack and swim to find him eating toast and coddled eggs.

—I wanted to call and say you had taken ill, she said.—But I didn't know who you were meeting with today. I figured it was best not to wake you.

—Good thing. Thank you, dear Karen. We'll go home this evening, all right? I can probably do the rest of my business from home.

—You don't remember what happened last night. Do you, Albert?

—No, he said grimly.—Guess that's enough rum for this trip.

—Finish your breakfast. I'll pack our things.

—You're an angel to put up with me. What's that on your lip, dear?

—This?

—Yes, he said, alarmed.—Doesn't it hurt? I hope you were careful when you went scuba diving.

A foreign couple at the table next to hers were calling for their check.

Karen looked down at the congealed brown goop at the bottom of her cup. She checked her wristwatch.

She looked across at the Granada. Only one doorman out there now.

After Karen's friend saw the pearls, she took to calling Albert, Prince Albert. Karen never told her about the incident with the belt.

—You mean you went to Jamaica and he didn't even take you dancing? He didn't get stoned even once? the friend said.—I guess Prince Albert will always be white bread.

Albert was a good enough looking man. But Karen understood fully why he seemed gray to other people. She understood why his employees, who truly liked and respected him, called him super straight. Why her friend had misidentified his hold over Karen.

—Well, he is rich and he ain't stingy, the friend noted.—God knows I never had a guy buy me a suit at Barney's every time I had to go to a meeting.

The gifts, the cash, the corner booths at the trendy restaurants. A woman putting up with no commitment because the perks were so good.

So maybe she was as mercenary as the next career girl. If only that explained it. If only it was about what he gave her, rather than what he wouldn't give her.

—And he does take you to fabulous places all the time, her friend said.—But don't tell me he's a great fuck, Karen. Because I won't believe you.

Karen blushed.

She left an enormous tip. So the waiter would remember her. She would be back.

K.

The bar conversation between Rufe and the two tourists from Albany had taken a raucous turn when Simon slid next to his old friend at the bar.

Without skipping a beat, however, Rufe turned and shouted to the bartender,—Give this sad hill-billy a Campari. At the same time he was squeezing Simon's neck hard with his fingers.

The tourists, both male, were in town to 'look around,' they said. Rufe had challenged them.—I have the feeling, gentlemen, you are after tits and ass. Which in turn had brought forth an explosion of denial, and then grudging admission.

The raucousness increased when Rufe said that after thinking it over, he realized he had made an error; and that they were, in fact, closeted gays who were into S&M.

Rufe said he could tell that by the cut of their clothes. One of the tourists, who was drunk, began to rip off his shirt to show Rufe that his back was free of whip marks or burns. His friend restrained him, but remonstrated with Rufe. And barbs flew back and forth.

Now, with the appearance of Simon, the raucousness died down. The tourists seemed to be sinking
like ships. Rufe turned his back on them and began
to circle Simon, then he pulled Simon's earlobe and
said,—You used to be a wild thang, Simone. Now
look at you. A jive ass burgher. A gladiolus from
Queens.

—Why, thank you, Rufe, for those kind words.

—We got a lot of places to go tonight.

—Not me, Rufe. Just two drinks and I'm home.

—Home is where the heart is.

—Bullshit.

—My, my, Simone. You are testy. Well, you know
what the trouble is. You been across the river too
long.

—What's going on with you, Rufe?

—Nothing much.

Simon gestured toward the tourists.—Still starting
trouble, I see.

—Ah, not trouble . . . just a bit of devilment.
Soon enough they will nail my little black ass to
the door of the governor's mansion. That's where
they're from, dear Simone, Albany.

—Indian country, said Simon.

—Exactly. Chirachua Apache. Where they party
on stewed puppy and turnips.

Simon put his bar face on . . . the one that is
thrust over the drink and stares at the far wall.

—Oh, I see that . . . I see that face, Simone . . .
deep in the hole . . . way down in the well. You

come with me and I swear you'll be up up up . . .
you'll get up . . . higher and higher. I could always
juice you up. You know that.

—Two drinks and home, Rufe. Sorry.

Rufe, angry now:—What is the matter with
everybody! What is going on? Who the hell do you
think you are? What are you saving? I haven't seen
you in six months and you show up like a cake of
bat shit. You don't want to drink with me, get the
fuck out of here.

—Take it easy, Rufe, take it easy.

The tourists left then. Rufe stared at their empty
stools. Then at Simon's profile. His attack on a
reluctant friend suddenly collapsed. Rufe realized
he really didn't care one way or the other if Simon
accompanied him on his rounds. It was Nettie he
wanted with him, as always. But she had laughingly
told him that she wanted the evening off.

—I took a peek in Jimmy's before I came here,
Simon said.

—That's nice, replied Rufe laconically, moving
closer to the bar and twirling the stem of his martini
glass. Then he added,—You see yo mama in there?

Rufe noticed Simon's lips press together tightly;
eyes steely. Simon shook his head, rueful, but then
gave the little man a facsimile of the sweetly indul-
gent smile that had melted so many hearts in the
past.

Rufe's irritation, however, would not dissolve.
What a drag this place is, he thought. But the night

was young; the night would get better. It always did.

Part 3

L.

Nettie waited for the light on South Street. She could see him huddled in the cold, without an overcoat, in front of the ancient ship moored in the harbor. She could see the box under his arm.

Suddenly he was gesturing wildly to her; palm out, fingers pointing up stiffly, like a traffic cop. It meant, Stay put. She waited. He crossed over, met her, and guided her into the bar on the corner – Sloppy Louie's, the famous old seafood pub. Like a dozen others she could think of right off the top of her head, it claimed to be probably the oldest drinking establishment in Manhattan.

They sat at the bar. He ordered a Jack Daniels on the rocks. She ordered red wine and water on the side. Once served, the proximity of the water glass and his bandaged face made her wince.

They had not yet said a word to each other.

He placed the box on the bar, removed the cover, pulled out the beret, and placed it in front of her.

This one was mustard-colored with a small black horse pin.

—It's lovely. Really.

She turned it over and over in her hands, then removed her own hat and fitted the beret onto her head. She stared at herself in the bar mirror. The color suited her.

—Are you hungry? he asked.

—Yes, she answered, surprised.

She wondered at the source of the odd gentleness between them.

—We could eat here, but they have a wonderful restaurant at that new hotel in Soho. I'm staying there. Will you join me?

—I thought you lived near Lincoln Center.

—Yes, I do. But that hotel always interested me. I used to go downtown and watch it being built. I always wondered what kind of people would stay there. So I checked in for a few days. He laughed self-deprecatingly.—That's what retired publishers with too much money do.

—What kind are they?

—Publishers, you mean?

—No. The people at the hotel.

—European for the most part.

She didn't reply. The old plan, rather, the old fantasy – after she took New York by storm, she would go to Paris and Milan . . . Dior . . . Versace . . . all gobbledy-gook now.

—I think I saw one of the bags you make, he said, smiling.

—Where?

—I got here early. I went to that shopping pier. There's a store called The Madeleine.

—Yes. They have several of my bags.

—Is it a lucrative line?

—I have to sell ten bags and ten hats a month to break even.

—Do you design them?

—I design, buy, cut, sew, market and deliver.

—Then you have a right to be hungry.

He took her discarded hat and placed it in the box. They walked to Water Street and caught a cab to the hotel on West Broadway. They sat close in the taxi, their shoulders touching. She felt no sense of intrusion nor enmity nor discomfort.

The restaurant in the hotel was up a flight of stairs. Little lights shining up through thick glass on each tread lit their way, making it seem that their shoes were sending off sparks as they walked up. There was a comfortable lounge attached to the restaurant. Square back, oversize chairs and sofas in gray plush. On the cubist tables in front of the seats were the remains of a tea service.

The food was *nouveau* American Gothic.

She had roast turkey with a strange squash and the most elusive, frothy cranberry sauce she'd ever tasted. He had *avant garde* pot roast. He ordered for her a half bottle of creamy white wine; for himself, more bourbon. They ate greedily but methodically, leaving nothing untouched. There seemed little need to speak. After all, wasn't this Armistice Day, the amicable end of their war?

—You turn eyes, he said over his pie.

She laughed.—South of Ninety-sixth Street, large handsome black women always turn eyes. That's what a friend of mine always says.

—Does it disturb you when people stare at you?

—Of course not. I was a model.

—What does disturb you?

—Bad faith and . . . She was about to say 'brutality' when she saw the bandage. So she said no more.

—Tell me what you think of this place, Nettie. He pronounced the 't's in her name like 'd's.

—The restaurant?

—No. The city.

—It is where I wanted to be.

—Have you ever thought of going home?

A shake of the head.

—Is the place you came from wretched?

—Wretched? I don't know about wretched. Choking, more like.

—And there are no nooses in New York?

—Yeah, a lot of them. But at night, if you have money, the rope loosens, and it can become velvet or silk. It sort of just caresses the neck.

She laughed at her own imagery. In a sense, she realized, she was taking Rufe's thoughts and prettifying them for this white man.

—Do you go to the theater?

—Sometimes.

—Movies?

—Sure.

—Concerts?

—Yes.

—Museums?

—I like the crafts museum. A gallery once in a while. What is going on – are you compiling a cultural profile of me?

—No, no, I don't mean it that way. He was chagrined, but continued:—Those concerts you go to . . . what kind of music?

She sipped her wine.—That Snoop Doggy Dog be one bad motherfucker, huh?

When she looked up, Albert Press had his eyes shut tight. She took the opportunity to study his bandage closely. The dressing had recently been changed. This one was not quite so big. But it seemed now to be digging into his face – taut, sucking. His teeth were clenched.

—Are you hurting, Albert?

—No, no, I'm fine. He opened his eyes.—Listen to me. I have another gift for you.

—This is too much.

—It's up in my room. Can you come with me there, now?

—No, I can't do that.

Why? There was obvious hurt in the question.— Are you afraid? Of me?

She didn't answer.

—Please don't be. It's as I said, I was in the grip of some kind of madness. This is me as I am – not the other.

—No. Look, Albert, this was all very nice. But I don't think we should try to take it any further. We climbed out of the pit, didn't we? We don't want to fall into another one.

—If you're frightened, we can get a bellhop to stay in the room with us.

—Why can't you just give it to me here?

—When you see it, you'll know why.

She sat in silence.

He leaned over the table and whispered urgently,—I will never harm you.

Nettie had a sudden flash of Louisa and herself in front of the TV late one night, many years ago, watching Steve McQueen kiss Faye Dunaway. It made her want to giggle and cry at the same time.

He walked into the room first.—Leave the door open if you wish.

She closed it.

He had taken a suite. There was a small kitchen, a hallway, a living room, and beyond that, a bedroom.

She followed him into the living room, stood there. He walked across the room, reached in and switched on the light in the other room.—Your gift is in there – on the bed, he said.—I'll wait out here.

Nettie went in.

On the comforter, not wrapped, was one of the most stunning dresses she had ever seen. Her size.

It was a Galliano – fire-engine-red wool and tight in the most perfect way. Whimsically finished in lush fur at the hem.

She called out:—I don't know what to say.

—Will you put it on?

This is getting very crazy, she thought. She closed the door, kicked off her boots, and slipped into the dress.

Then she appeared in the doorway. Albert Press was standing by the window. He was staring at her. She smiled, walked up one side of the living room and down the other, then quickly, on the diagonal, back toward the bedroom.

She heard an animal cry. Turned in fear. He was bent over, holding on to the windowsill.

She rushed to his side, then stepped away, startled.

He was now grasping at his crotch, trying to stop his ejaculation, which spread out over his pants.

Suddenly she was overcome with compassion for this man. She buried her face in his sandy hair and tried to soothe him.

When it was over, he staggered to the sofa.—I'm sorry. Oh, God, I'm sorry.

She ran into the bedroom, pushed into her boots, threw on her overcoat, and rushed out through the door.

M.

—You keeping something from me, honey? Rufe asked wickedly.

—I tell you everything, Nettie replied.

—Then how does a poor little working girl like yourself get a dress like that?

—I have my sources.

—I do hope you're not turning tricks.

Nettie kissed Rufe on the cheek.

He said,—At least I know it wasn't the beret freak who came to my office.

—How can you be so sure?

—Oh, honey, please. You're such a country girl at heart. When hat freaks cross over, they go into shoes, not dresses. Besides, I must've scared that creep out of his brown sugar hard-on. I never heard from him again. Of course, you no doubt have many other secret admirers; they see you across a smoky bar . . . they lust . . . they interrogate bartenders . . . and then they come to me in the hope that I can provide them a taste of the fruit from the garden of Nettie.

They were drinking in a new place in the East

Village, on Third Street. The top of the bar was silvery. The patrons silent and slinky. Every soul in black, customers and staff alike.

—You're acting strange, lady. You're looking strange.

—It's the dress, Rufe. You just never saw me in designer red before.

There were flickering candles on the bar. The couple in the corner, at a table, were entwined. They were either in love or high, possibly both. The man looked Arab. The woman was golden-haired and emaciated. A beautiful black polar fleece short jacket circled her shoulders. The music – Ray Charles at the piano – seemed to weave in and out of their supine embrace.

Rufe noticed her looking.—Do you like them, Nettie?

—I think I do.

—You sure there's nothing you want to tell old Uncle Pleasant?

She opened a pack of Kool Mild 100s and lit one off the candle on the bar.—A confession, you mean.

—If you wish.

—What about a question? A philosophical question.

—Honey, there is nothing on earth I like better than a real down-home, in your face, whole ball of wax, cut you no slack, in-perpetuity puzzler. He snapped his fingers loudly, grinning,—Hell, baby, look at what I'm drinking. Extra-dry Beefeater –

straight up – no fruit. Is that the libation of a man who don't like philosophical questions?

Nettie took a deep drag and shifted her weight on the stool.

—What do you think of white men, Rufe?

—Say what?

—White men. What do you think of them?

Rufe burst out laughing.—That's the question? I love it! But you've got to clarify just a bit.

—What is there to clarify?

—Are you talking about white men between the ages of pubescence and senescence who are domiciled in the continental United States and have intact genitalia which they use from time to time?

—Yes.

—Put to heterosexual use?

—Yes.

—Aha. The field is now narrowed considerably, he replied, and sat down. Rufe actually took a seat. Things were getting serious.

—I think, my dear, that a certain kind of white boy is mighty cute.

—I'm serious, Rufe.

—Okay. To be more precise, smart white men tend to be crazy. Stupid white men tend to be either sweet or murderous. This is a general law with few exceptions. One of those exceptions is the category of tall thin white men who wear corduroy suits. They are, in a sense, mystical niggers. And honey, they are dangerous.

—That's not helpful.

—I didn't know you needed help. I thought this was a philosophical question. Hypothetical. An abstraction.

She realized how ridiculous it had been to ask Rufe such a question. It was jejune in the extreme. Meaningless. But she knew her eyes had sought out the faces of the patrons in this bar because they were white. And she knew she was somehow, in some way, tying the face of Albert Press to theirs.

What had happened in that hotel room was still very much with her – but it made no more sense now than when it occurred. She knew exactly what had happened to Albert. It was herself she was confused about. She didn't know what had happened to her. The man had cried out in anguish and ejaculated. Premature or autonomous ejaculation. He had not masturbated nor been masturbated this time. He had just watched her walk. Why hadn't she asked Rufe a question about that?

Above all, what nagged at her and what made her cycle back and forth between depression and triumph was how she had reacted.

Why had she felt such compassion for the man?

Why had she touched him, literally snuggled against him in a gesture of consolation?

Why, in fact, had she agreed to meet him again? Did she really want to end it? Did she really crave another expensive gift? Why had she gone to his hotel room? Why had she tried on the dress? Why was she wearing it now?

She was not a child. She was not a virgin. She had slept with men, with white men, with black men, and with a woman. She was respectful of Eros in all its normality and perversity.

But this man was not like any of those other partners. This was a man who had elicited in her murder and degradation and unbelievable tenderness.

She crushed her cigarette out in a fury.

—I want to dance, she announced.

—Go ahead.

—Not in here, fool. In a disco.

—Honey, discos went out with Lionel Ritchie.

—Okay, so they don't call them that anymore. But you know what I meant. I meant a place where I could dance. You must know one, Rufe.

—Sure I do. It's funky, it's reggae, and it's in Chelsea.

—Take me there.

Rufe smiled and said in a bad Bob Marley accent:—Why not, rude girl? It is Jah. And Jah is reggae. And reggae is the beat of the human heart.

N.

Detective Prego circled the long table as Albert Press slowly went through the remainder of the warrant photos. Prego was uncomfortable with what was happening. Press was sober this time, that was for sure. But the process was still bogus somehow. Prego could always pick up on these things. This man was going through the photos too methodically. He was spending the same amount of time on each. It made no kind of sense.

In some way, this Albert Press was hustling him. But why?

Prego went back around the table and sat down opposite him. He asked,—Anything interesting?

—Not yet, Albert said without looking up.

—Funny. The last time you were here you picked out three girls in the first five minutes.

—True, admitted Albert, still not looking up.— But as you said, I was probably inebriated at the time.

The detective did not respond. He studied the man going through the warrants. Prego was proud of his intuition; he lived and died by it. In this case, however, it was not working at all, except in the sense that he knew Press was lying about what really went down in that bar, that night. Prego knew about bar slashings, oh yes, he knew a lot about them.

First of all, they never took place in bars like the Rouge Lounge, and rarely in working-class neighborhood bars, either.

They usually occurred in transient bars or bars on DMZ lines. Bars which bordered different ethnic and racial neighborhoods. Or bars situated close to bus and railroad terminals. Like the ones on Eighth or Ninth Avenue, near the Port Authority Bus Terminal, or in Washington Heights, or Atlantic Avenue in Brooklyn, or Jamaica Avenue in Queens.

And the slashings themselves usually followed one or two patterns: the most prevalent being simply an escalation of an innocent conversation into an argument. It could start with something as banal as the evaluation of a single play in a baseball game on the bar TV . . . or a single news event . . . or the accuracy of a memory of some past event . . . or a comment about a bar patron who had just walked out.

There was another category, not so common, but a statistical reality. That was where the slasher was psychotic. He is sitting alone and drinking. Halfway down the bar another is drinking alone. The psycho simply gets up, walks over to the victim, and cuts his face open. No words. No warning. No reason except for the demons in the crazy man's brain.

What happened in the Rouge Lounge fit none of these scenarios. Oh, sure, the woman could have been psycho. Her act really could have been triggered by a put-down of her favorite movie star. A crazy, and a black crazy at that, could be set off by anything.

Prego studied the man's face intently. This latest bandage was the smallest yet. The wound was obviously healing well. He wondered why he kept thinking of the incident as a bar slashing. It really wasn't — no knife or razor had been used. The weapon had been a glass of water.

A possibility intruded. Wild, but possible. This man, Albert Press, was the psychotic. And the wound had been self-inflicted. He had smashed the glass against his own face. Maybe a masochistic macho thing to impress a woman who wouldn't give him a chance. Look, I am tough. I can take pain. I'll happily self-mutilate. And the woman runs out in terror. Who wouldn't?

Prego realized even as he had the thought how utterly stupid that theory was. He could just imagine himself taking that one to the brass: Yep, this one's all solved. Looks like this rich white guy was trying to impress a girl. Or maybe commit suicide by slicing his own throat with a glass of water. The woman sitting next to him was scared shitless and ran for her life.

No. The man sitting across from him was off the wall, but not deranged. A garden variety alkie. Prego had seen enough of them to know. So Press was a drunk and a liar and Prego didn't have very much use for him. But he had an undeniable compassion for that kind of cripple. Some cops pitied junkies; for some it was hookers; he cast a forgiving eye on drunks. Press, like his drugging, whoring counterparts, lied every minute of every hour. Prego knew that was to be taken for granted. And in fact he was looking for a way to help Albert Press out of the lie.

Suddenly Albert groaned, and sat back in his chair. He ran both hands through his thick hair.

—Find something?

—No, nothing. The weariness just came over me. All the sadness. I mean, these women.

—They do the crime, Mr. Press. The law says they have to do the time.

—Yes, yes. I understand that. Believe me, detective, I am not a bleeding heart.

—I never said you were.

—But I don't think I'm going to find her here.

—You know, I don't think so either.

—It's apples and oranges, detective.

—How so?

—I mean, one thing I do know is that the woman at the bar is absolutely unlike the women wanted on these warrants.

—How can you know that?

—I don't know. I just do.

—Do you think she might attack another man in another bar during another movie conversation?

—Oh, I would say no.

—Do you think, maybe, she had a sexual fantasy about this movie actor – Irons? A really strong thing for him. And your comment offended her so much that she lashed out? She'd have done the same thing no matter who was sitting there, maybe. Think that's possible, Mr. Press?

—It's possible, Press admitted.

—From what I understand, Mr. Press, you publish travel guidebooks – or used to.

—That's correct.

—Did your company ever do a New York City guide?

—Of course.

—Was the Rouge Lounge in it?

—I don't know. I doubt it.

—You have a co-op near Lincoln Center, don't you?

—Yes.

—Where do you drink around there?

—A bar on Columbus.

—What's the name?

—I can never remember it.

—Do you pick up women in that bar?

—I never pick up women. In any bar.

Prego smiled. He knew that if he kept on questioning Albert Press, he would unearth sixteen tons

of little white lies. But so what? None of them
would be worth a damn in this case.

O.

She breakfasted on half an orange, one piece of toast with margarine, and a cup of coffee. It was an abstemious breakfast for a woman who was always hungry in the morning. But it was from habit – she no longer dieted.

Oh, when the weight had begun to accumulate, she had gone on diet after diet. One more extreme than the other. Nothing helped. Her body would not go thin again. The diets did slow the increase of her increase. And that gave her the clue that something else was happening to her, something other than just pounds.

The answer, of course, turned out to be in the genes. All the women in Nettie's family were large . . . not fat, but particularly large, broad-shouldered, wide-hipped, long-legged, big-footed. And, anomalously, small-breasted.

And she had simply started to enter her destiny at a relatively young age, at the very worst time possible, considering the career she had chosen.

After breakfast, because the heat was coming up

fine, she got right to work, still in her quilted bathrobe.

The task was to finish off five bags. All that had to be done was to fasten the cloth shoulder straps to the bags themselves. She didn't need the machine for that. The small hand-held stitch gun was sufficient; it was like using a stapler.

When she finished she drew a bath. Her body ached from the dancing. It had been fun, but she really didn't know what she was doing. Rufe had gone absolutely bananas, like a twisty dervish gnome whirling through the music. She had never been much of a reggae fan, never paid much attention to it, and what she had heard of it was slow and lyrical. This on the other hand was very fast and pounding, druggy but manic, and the dancers were young, oh so young. But few of them could equal Rufe, once he got into gear.

The phone rang at 10 AM. She knew exactly who it was. She had been expecting the call and she felt nothing but calm.

The moment she picked up, Albert launched into a monologue.

—I was too embarrassed to call you until now. I was so goddamn ashamed of myself, I wanted to crawl into a drainpipe and just rust away. I don't know what happened, Nettie. It was seeing you in that dress. When I saw the dress on Madison Avenue, I had to get it for you. I could envision you in it. But the reality of you wearing it . . .

when you walked out of the bedroom . . . when you walked past me . . . you were so beautiful, so exquisite, so desirable . . . I just . . .

—Came apart, she supplied.

He laughed derisively. — Exploded! Like an adolescent boy. And you were so kind, in spite of it.

She didn't answer.

—Are you there, Nettie? Are you listening?

—Yes.

—Please have lunch with me. Today. At that hotel again. Please let me see you again.

—When?

—At two. Will two be okay?

—Where will I meet you?

—In the lobby. I'll be waiting.

She felt as though she had no say in the matter, and she didn't mind. It was good to be caught up with the unexpected, wasn't it? That's what it was all about, according to Rufe. You were supposed to let yourself get caught up. Fifty-fifty. Those were the odds. Plenty of things had worked out just fine when she'd simply allowed herself to be pulled along.

She hung up the phone, imagining for a second that the scent of his hair was on the mouthpiece.

She walked to the window and stared down onto East Broadway. The street was always packed with people. She saw two men carrying sides of fresh-killed suckling pig into one of the restaurants. She loved the Chinese, they were direct – primal – and yet so sophisticated at the same time.

She smiled. How many times had this man apologized to her? Dozens?

Nettie arrived at the hotel on time. Albert wasn't in the lobby. She located him in the hotel bar and the moment he saw her he began to babble; how good she looked in the mustard-colored beret, and how he had never seen a woman wear a hat with such élan.

She ordered some wine to shut him up. He said,
—You know, we can eat at the bar.

—That would be nice, she said. So they settled in. No one else was there except for the bartender. She didn't know how many Jack Daniels Albert had already consumed. He ordered a hamburger. She ordered the cheese and winter fruit platter.

—Are your folks alive? he asked.

—My mother is.

—Do you have brothers and sisters?

—No. Just me.

—Where are you people from?

—What do you mean? I told you where I grew up.

—I mean in the South. Before your family moved north.

—I don't know. Alabama, I think.

—And before that?

She laughed.—You mean Africa?

—Yes.

—I haven't the slightest idea.

—Do you have any other friends in the city? Other than that little man from the temp agency?

—When I was modeling I had a lot of friends. Then I drifted away. Or we all drifted away.

—That's sad.

—Why do you ask me so many questions? Why are you always conducting an interrogation?

—I don't mean it to sound that way. Look, please ask me whatever you want to know.

She had no questions. He said: —I'm a bit sheepish announcing this, but I have another gift for you.

—What's the matter with you, man? Why do you keep doing that?

—Believe me, it's not a dress. It's . . . well . . . just something rare and beautiful. I saw it and I indulged myself.

She picked at her cheese platter. This lunch seemed to be going badly.

—Let me show it to you. It won't take long. He called out to the bartender,—We'll be right back. Could you cover my burger?

He held out his hand. She took it. They went to the room. They walked together into the bedroom.

—There, on the bed, in that bag.

She sat down on the bed and pulled at the object. Heavy.

She uttered a sharp cry of astonishment.—Oh, Lord, it's magnificent, she whispered.

—Yes, yes. I knew you would like it.

—It must have cost a fortune.

He waved her concern away.

Nettie ran her hands over the bright-colored hand-woven wool blanket with the symmetrical lightning bolt designs.

It was either Navajo or Hopi, she knew. It had to be at least eighty, maybe a hundred years old. And the design and the color and workmanship were spectacular.

—You can wear it downstairs, he said.

—This isn't the kind of thing you wear, is it? I'll look like a squaw, she said.

—Or like a queen of the *pueblos*, he replied.

She stood up and wrapped the blanket around her shoulders. She walked to one wall and turned, presenting it.—How does it look?

What happened next, happened very fast. He was down on his knees in front of her. He carefully opened her slacks and pulled them down; then her pantyhose. She didn't resist. She didn't help.

He said something again and again, but she couldn't hear what it was. He buried his faced in between her legs. His lips and tongue found her clitoris. He sucked her gently and then his lips just held her.

She did not feel intense sexual excitement. It was something unexpected, hard to define.

There was a progression, a leisurely progression, but the set did not change.

And then came the quietest orgasm.

She remained exactly where she was, standing against the wall, the blanket on her shoulders.

Albert Press was collapsed on the floor. She bent down and tousled his hair.

She folded the blanket carefully over the chair back. Then they went down to finish their lunch.

Part 4

P.

Rufe was working himself into a strange old Negro monologue.—Miss Nettie looks sad. It's very bad when Miss Nettie is sitting at a fine bar and weeping bitter silent tears. It is a bad, bad thing.

She cut it off at the pass.—I'm not sad. I'm thinking.

—No time for thinking, lady. The pot is boiling. We are going to have one wild time tonight. We are going to party whilst the bad moon rises.

—Then why are we in Fanelli's? she asked, giving him the needle.

—Yeah, you're right. This place depresses me now. Soho depresses me now. Because I remember when Fanelli's was like a jambalaya. Now it's a spinach quiche. And Soho is a green salad. So here I be, sinking into a deep depression, like you, baby. But I don't want to drown. So I know the next spot will be better. And it will rev up. I know it's going to be a long and good night.

She reached out and grabbed his small face with her hands.—Listen to me, Rufe. I met someone.

—Oh?

—I just wanted you to know.

—So now I know. He shook her hands off his face. He made the sign of the cross on her brow.— Fuck in peace.

Then he laughed. He felt much better. He ordered another martini.

Suddenly he leaned forward and cursed.—Is it that freak, Nettie! Is it?

She didn't answer.

He did one of his furious little pirouettes.—That dress! Of course. That fucking dress you were wearing the other night. It was from him. Oh, Nettie! What has happened to your fucking sense, girl?

She held up her hand to caution him that he should go no further.

—You bullshitting your Uncle Pleasant, Nettie? You didn't meet 'someone.' You met an old-fashioned sugar daddy. You ring his bell and he'll fill your closet. What else did he give you? Is that freak going to buy you the world?

—He's not a freak, she said softly.

—Tell me, honey. Speak to me. Give me the facts. Ease your Aunt Rufe's mind so she don't think you turned into another little housing-project whore on the make.

Her fingers tightened around the water glass on the bar. Then she pulled her hand away quickly. She looked at Rufe. She wanted to ease his anger. She didn't know what his anger was about. Why did he keep calling Albert a freak? He'd only met him once, and briefly at that. She wanted to tell him how kind the man was. How his gifts were not an attempt to buy her. How the gifts meant nothing. She found herself unable to say a word. She knew why. Because then she would have to tell Rufe what had happened in the Rouge Lounge and at Trio's. That would shame her. Not just shame her – it would solidify Rufe's opinion. Nettie felt weak, abandoned, boxed in. She began to rub cruelly at her forehead.

Rufe moved right beside her.—I got a big mouth, honey. Too early in the evening. Don't listen to anything I say.

—I'm tired, Rufe. I need to sleep.

—It's the soaps, honey. It's Manhattan. Life is a sweet and sour soap. Fuck who you want, Nettie. I treasure you. Don't go home.

—Let me go home, Rufe. Don't be mad.

—I can't be mad at you. Sure, go home. Get some rest. We'll talk another time. We'll party another time. Go home.

Nettie walked through the old wooden door and did not look back. Rufe fiddled with his martini glass, cursing himself for his outburst. Beautiful Nettie has met someone. So why didn't he just keep his mouth shut? She could take care of herself. And who isn't a freak? Imagine Yours Truly calling anybody else a freak.

He groaned. I define freak, he thought. I am the queen of freak. I am the Beefeater freak.

Flowers, he thought. Maybe I will send her flowers. And perfumed condoms for her man. That ludicrous thought perked him up.

Q.

Nettie was in Bloomingdale's. It was noon. Bloomingdale's was the only place she knew of that carried the eau de parfum that was her signature scent. It came from a shop near the Bois de Boulogne, where she had never been. She rode up and down the narrow escalators which, depending on her mood, could be anxiety-provoking. The Bloomingdale's escalators could feel so constricting, like wearing patent leather shoes that were a size too small.

Not this time. This time she felt good. It had been a long time since she had just wandered around like this — not since she had first come to New York.

She left the store, walked to Madison Avenue and headed north. She turned into Barney's, looked around and walked out. She was moving into her imperious mode, head held a bit too high, an expression around the mouth that made other women grudgingly concede her good looks but then comment to each other that she must be a bitch. Many of the models and ex-models she used to know would fall into that mode. It would happen when they drank too much and ate too little – a kind of silly postural spillover from the runway into the real world.

But Nettie no longer had that emaciated beauty, and when in the thick of that mode she just frightened people.

She had never been able to place any of her bags and hats in the Madison Avenue stores. Her merchandise simply wasn't pricey enough. And she hated all the hardware on uptown accessories.

She kept walking uptown on Madison. It was a windless cold sunny day. There was a weariness to the street. She could feel it. But that was to be expected after the hysteria of Christmas and New Year. Nettie knew the pattern: in the early spring many stores would fold.

At Seventy-ninth Street she began to grow tired and looked for a place to stop, to rest. At Eighty-first and Madison she walked into a pub. That was the only word listed on the canopy, simply, pub – with a time-weathered menu posted on the front door.

The inside was clean but gloomy with small tables covered by red and white checked oilcloth. Blessedly, there was no music playing. She felt exceedingly comfortable in that quiet place.

She quickly realized why. The few patrons in there were immediately identifiable WASPs, and Nettie always felt comfortable with them. It was the ethnics in New York who made her nervous, and often her own people. What was it about white white people – Anglos – that put her at her ease? Maybe it was that nothing too complicated was likely to happen between them and herself. Or maybe it was the quaintness of the things they seemed to concern themselves with. At any rate, it tended to cut misunderstandings down to a minimum.

The waiter was a slow-moving old man. She ordered the pub's specialty – honey chicken – and then sipped water and smoked. She didn't order anything from the bar.

The old waiter placed a basket of bread down on the table alongside a saucer with three tabs of butter. How bad the bread is in New York restaurants, she thought, flashing on her mother's sour milk biscuits, those miniature moons – she and Louisa slathering them with butter and dipping them in fake maple syrup. They put sugar in the cornbread up here, too.

Nettie tore off a corner of a rye bread roll, buttered it and began to chew. She realized at the same instant that she had become wet between her legs. Period starting? Or was it her imagination? She put the bread down. She could feel his mouth between her legs, that slow incessant pressure. Not finding the spot till the very end. It was an erotic flashback, and anticipation of the next time, when it would be much better, when they would really make love.

How good it would feel when Albert made her come.

Louisa had grown up so fast. She would tell Nettie which of her lovers 'could fuck good' and which could not. Even today, the phrase made Nettie blush.

But Louisa was talking only about the mechanics. You don't think that way when you're in love. When you're in love you feel cared for, beautifully confused. Yes, that's what she was undergoing; she was lovesick. But not five minutes later she was grabbed at the throat by the old devil – I am alone. I am bloody alone. There is no help. I will be hurt. I will not be safe.

Beads of sweat flowered on her forehead. Her ramrod posture vanished.

She wanted to see Albert. She wanted to talk to strange Albert Press. She had been tempted to say to Rufe:—He isn't a freak. He's fucked up. But he's not a freak. Nettie winced.

There were hundreds of things she wanted to tell Albert . . . confessions . . . pains gone unsoothed . . . but somehow she could not manage to speak to him from her heart. She had never said two intimate words to the man. There had been his tentative interrogations of her, that's all. But no doubt now there was intimacy between them. It was beyond question. And just under the surface, in that thin membrane beneath the peel, there was something else. Something she craved.

She looked around. There was a payphone by the bar.

Her fingers broke off another piece of bread. She buttered it feverishly but didn't eat it. Instead, she left the table, went to the phone, and dialed Albert's hotel.

There was no answer in the room. She asked that the call be switched to the bar phone. The bartender picked up. Nettie inquired if Mr. Press was there.

—Yes. Hold on. The phone was passed.

He recognized Nettie's voice immediately.—I was sitting here, he said,—and thinking of what brought us together. It was not fate, you beautiful, kind woman. It was not fate at all. It was Manhattan. And the waters that surround it. We were washed up together on the same wave.

—There are no waves in the Hudson, Albert, Nettie replied.

The old waiter had shown up with the honey chicken. He was looking around for her, confused. She caught his eye and motioned for him to just leave it on the table.

Albert panicked.—Are you there? Are you there?

—Yes.

—Where?

—In a pub on Madison.

—So now you agree. Right? We are both in a bar. We are waiting for each other. Like still waters. I am an anti-poet, he called loudly into the phone, sounding almost crazy.

Was he crazy? Panicked, she thought for a moment that she had better hang up right then and there. Run. Disconnect her home phone. But then she realized, he was just drunk.

His voice had calmed, anyway.—Wild waters, Nettie. Manhattan. The prow of the boat clearing the surf. He laughed too much again.—What a boat, Nettie! What surf! Please come here now. I ask you in all humility and love.

—Wait for me, she said.

She hung up, and fumbled for a twenty-dollar bill. She thought, To hell with the honey chicken. And God bless WASP hang-outs.

R.

Rufe sat up in bed. He knew he was in a hotel, but he didn't, for the moment, know where.

It was a stinking, tiny room with a single print of a rearing horse on the wall. The wall itself was painted destroyer gray. There were two windows, locked and cloudy.

At the far wall, next to the door and the dresser, was a slashed blue easy chair.

Seated in it was a naked young Hispanic man in a turned-around Chicago Cubs hat. A Walkman in his lap, he was wearing the earphones. His body, though narrow, was heavily muscled and tattooed. He was quite beautiful.

—What time is it? Rufe asked. The young man was too absorbed in his music to hear.

Rufe studied the available light from the windows and ascertained it was about noon.

At that point, he knew exactly where he was and how he had come to be there.

He was in a Bowery flophouse. Or at least a flophouse close to the Bowery. Forty dollars the night. And that beautiful Latino angel in the ugly blue chair had cost him a hundred dollars.

He had picked him up outside a bar on Walker Street; maybe 2:30 A.M. The boy had been happily pissing off the loading dock of an old factory. A high arc of urine gleaming in the night.

They had walked east together, he skipping, the boy with a Riker's Island swagger. Due east in the cold dark night, and on that walk all those martinis had destroyed caution. It was Nettie's fault. She shouldn't have abandoned him in Fanelli's.

On Elizabeth Street he had pulled the boy into a doorway and sucked his sweet cock. He had lapped at it, swallowed it, pacified it as though the meat were a thrashing predator caught in a net.

As the boy came in his mouth he had smashed Rufe with his fist on the back of the head and Rufe fell beneath him. The boy laughed and put on his Walkman.

They went to the flophouse and the boy fucked him hard on the chair – Rufe squatting on it, like a little black dog.

Rufe swung his feet onto the floor. His clothes were scattered all over. Where had the boy slept? Had he slept?

With an outlaw child like this, he knew, he was playing Russian Roulette. But he felt good, almost sly. He was in no hurry; no place to go; he had told his boss he wouldn't be in for a couple of days. She cared not at all whether he showed up, as long as he kept bringing in the accounts.

He dressed slowly. There was no shower or sink in the room. Only a toilet. He felt the boy's eyes on him. He smiled. The boy was watching him dress, watching his clothes, taking him in in a way Rufe could not understand but surely could appreciate. The boy's body bounced a bit to the tune he was hearing through the headset and with each tensing and relaxing, the muscles of his stomach and the tattoos flexed.

Rufe knotted his tie. He could read the tattoos now, over the boy's nipples: *Hot* over one, *Cold* over the other. And on his right arm was a two-headed snake spitting twin streams of venom. *Bad to the bone* was lettered like an aureole above the heads.

Oh my, Little Rufe, he whispered to himself, Why do you always end up with the sweet killers?

—We eat? Rufe asked him. The kid signaled: he couldn't hear.

Rufe made a gesture – one hand scooping food into the mouth.

The boy smiled. Then he dressed and they walked down the smelly stairs together like promenaders in *Saratoga Trunk*.

S.

She was breathless when she slid beside him at the hotel bar. He beamed at her. Shook his head from side to side in wonderment. He seemed over-whelmed by the fact that she had arrived, that she was there.

She reached over, picked up his glass, and drained the Jack Daniels, sifting the ice out with her teeth.

He kissed the hand that held the glass.

—Manhattan is an island, she said.

—Washed by waves, he said.

—The surf is rising, she said.

He sucked her thumb.—What surf? What island? he asked, then stood up and shouted to the bar-tender for two more Jack Daniels.

When they arrived, the couple gulped them down.

Nettie felt her head begin to pound. She could not tolerate whisky.

—We can move to Inwood, Nettie. At the north tip of the island. We will buy an apartment house and stand up there in the snow, on the roof, and stare down at the ice floes on the Hudson as they drift south with bedraggled eagles on them.

His hand slid around the back of her stool, onto her ass. She leaned back into it.

—Let's go up, Albert. Take me up.

They reeled away from the bar and into the elevator. The moment they stepped inside the room, he pulled her sweater up, ripped off her bra and began to suck her nipples wildly. Nettie yelled,— Fuck me now, Albert. Please fuck me now.

But he stepped back, suddenly grown solemn and shy.

—First you must see what I brought you.

—No, please! No more gifts, Albert.

She began to pull off her clothes.

—No, wait . . . stop. I can't do that, Nettie.

He clamped down on her fumbling fingers.

Then, releasing her, he rushed to the closet and pulled out a garment, lay it lovingly on the carpet.

—What have you done?

—Look at it, Nettie, he said.—Have you ever seen anything so beautiful?

It was a wedding gown. A magnificent pouf of ivory tulle and ribbons, with an endless train.

He grabbed at her.—Lay down on it, Nettie.

—No. I don't want to.

—But you must. Please lay on it.

—Albert . . . why . . .

But she could not withstand his urgency. He helped her remove the rest of her clothing. And then he helped her onto the floor, into the folds of the dress.

Nude now, she turned on her side, it was an involuntary motion, and looked up at him through her lashes. He was staring at her worshipfully. He took off his own garments then and knelt beside her. Locking eyes with her, he reached over to the spot on the floor where his jacket had fallen. From the pocket he slowly extracted a single strand of pearls. Stupefied, Nettie watched while he wound the pearls around her wrist and used them to anchor her arm to a chair leg. It was no surprise when he duplicated the gesture, extracting a second strand from his pocket, and fixing her other arm to a second chair leg. Next, he placed his hands gently on her stomach, palms down, and held them there as if taking a seismic reading.

Then the strange licking began and she could do nothing to stop it. Or, would do nothing to stop it. The truth was, she could have freed herself at any time.

Part 5

T.

She was cautious when she opened the door to her loft. And she opened it just a smidgen. No one ever knocked on her door at this time of night, except lost Chinese immigrants. It couldn't be Albert; he was away for a few days, in Boston, doing some consulting.

Nettie was startled to see Rufe outside the door, and delighted.

—Are you going to just keep on looking at me? Didn't you ever see anyone this pretty? Let me in, doll-face.

She slid the door open and embraced him, then walked him into the loft and deposited him on the sofa.

—I have drinks. I have food. I have cookies. What do you want, Rufe?

He ignored her offerings.—Where the hell have you been? he spat out.—You don't call. You don't talk to me. You just disappear. What the fuck's going on, Nettie?

She sat down on the sofa beside him, her hand on his knee. She had acted abominably, she knew, but she had simply been unable to tell him the truth.

Now there was no way out.

—Rufe, listen, I'm not going to be able to make night rounds with you anymore.

—Fine. All you had to do was tell me. What was I going to do? Commit suicide?

He was trying to be cool and rational, she realized. But the hurt was on his voice like a rash.

—I just don't have the energy anymore, Rufe. It happens like that. I'm in love, Rufe. And the man loves me.

Rufe grinned and said,—Freak Town.

She slapped him hard in the face, then sat back in horror at what she had done and began to babble an abject apology.

He kept grinning at her, cutting off her ravings with the laconic question—So you love him, did you say?

—Yes.

—And he you?

—Yes.

—And there is peace in the realm.

—Yes.

—And he's stopped giving you gifts.

—Yes, she lied.

He appeared to accept it with equanimity; as a kind of sad fact of life. But then his eyes began to scan the loft. And they alighted on the exercise barre at the far side of the room – the barre she had bought years ago, in the throes of a renewed belief that she was going to get thin again.

There were garments draped over the high-polished wood of the barre.

He sauntered over. He picked up the red dress and inspected it silently with a mock critical expression, then replaced it.

He pulled the blanket off, evaluated it in the same manner, and replaced it.

Still not speaking, he popped open the door of the nearby wardrobe. With the wedding dress, he was lavish in his mugging.—Just a little frock you keep handy in case someone drops in for tea, eh? Pathetic liar, his expression said.

Rufe took the dress off its hanger and laid it too across the barre, arranging it meticulously, deep into his routine of prissed lips and raised eyebrows. The queen's eunuch courtier showing off the sumptuous fabrics which, at untold peril to himself, he had crossed oceans and braved all manner of brigands to bring to her chamber.

When the show was over, he made as if to come back to the sofa to join her. But he stopped at the coffee table, see-sawing his red cashmere muffler back and forth across his neck.

—So it's good, huh?

How filthy that sounded.

Nettie looked away.

—He does you real good, huh?

—It's not like that, Rufe.

—Not like what?

—I mean I'd be lying if I said it was like getting good and laid. Old-fashioned fucking. Raucous fucking. Like you used to say. It isn't . . . like that. But it's— She faltered.

—You don't have to tell me a thing, Nettie.

—You know that's not true.

He waited.

—He – licks me. That's part of it. No, wait, not just licks me. I mean all over. Outside. And inside. I want more, but he . . . won't.

Rufe didn't say a word.

—I know what you think of him, Rufe. I know he is a bit strange. And it's true I want him to – I want the old-fashioned thing, the regular thing. But he won't. And that first time he did it? I admit I was repelled. But then – then I realized it was about love. Between me and him, Rufe. You understand? You understand how it's about love between us? No, I can see you don't.

So, Sweet Fucked Up Nettie's on Catfish Row at last, thought Rufe.

—Look, I am really sorry I slapped you, but we are not 'freak town.' We are two people who— She couldn't finish. She stared down blankly at her hands.

There was a tune going round in his head: 'What do he want with Bess?'

—What's so funny, Rufe? What are you grinning like that for?

134

He shook his head.

Rufe's agitation was now so severe that he had to fold his own hands in his lap to keep them from shaking. He was suddenly very afraid for her. He was a sexually sophisticated man. Yes, the tongue could be a thing of beauty. He knew that. He had tongued and been tongued in every which way. But he had heard of what she was talking about only once before. In the army. A sergeant who had spent two tours in Vietnam – his name was Cotton. He had told Rufe about a strange brothel in Saigon where one paid a great deal of money to have young Vietnamese girls do what this Albert was doing to Nettie.

—Coffee would be nice, he said.

She nodded and walked slowly to the kitchen. He watched her go, she of the broad back and the stately carriage and luscious hips, the hem of her thick bathrobe almost touching the floor. My beautiful Nettie is in trouble, he thought. Very big trouble.

He waited until she was out of view. And then he walked quickly to her desk. He found her address book. He began to leaf feverishly through the pages. He had to find someone who could talk to her. Her mother maybe, or that friend – Louisa – whom Nettie was always talking about so bitingly.

—What are you doing?

Rufe turned. She was standing at the entrance to the kitchen holding two bags of coffee beans.

He dropped the book back onto the desk.—I'm looking for somebody to call.

—Call about what? she boomed.

—You. I'm getting help for you, Nettie.

—Help! You stupid little man. For the first time in my life, I don't need your help.

Rufe shook his head.—Who would ever have thought that after all these years of drinking with me in the garden spots of the western world, you would end up a stupid bitch?

Her explosion was all finished. She responded quite softly,—Go now, Rufe. Stay away from me.

—What did you say?

—Get out, Rufe. Go and choke on your faggot dreams.

He smiled, bowed a little bow, and walked out.

U.

Rufe did not make his usual rounds after the ugly altercation in Nettie's apartment, nor did he go to work the next morning. He sat in his pleasant Grove Street apartment, thinking. This was unusual. He did most of his best thinking at his office desk or on a barstool. In fact, he spent very little time at home.

One wall of his living room was exposed brick surrounding a fireplace. It was this room which contained his treasure, a brilliant counterfeit of an eighteenth-century country dining-room table. He had first sighted it in a fancy Bleecker Street antiques store. It was priced at $16,000. Rufe had pointed out to the owner that one of the small sliding drawers underneath the table was made out of cleverly disguised machine-processed plywood — a bit difficult for French peasants in the eighteenth century. The shop owner had taken $900 for the table. Now Rufe was not sure whether it was counterfeit or not. It might well be an authentic frame that had been rebuilt.

Rufe made himself one egg over easy in the small

kitchen, then carried the pan back to the table and proceeded to consume the egg slowly.

He was hung over and he couldn't account for that. After all, he had had only a couple of vodkas here in the house last night. He had gone right home after the visit with Nettie. And he had slept the sleep of the just.

He wiped the run-out yoke from the pan with a piece of bread and just sat there in his pajama bottoms. Sun was flooding into the living room. The apartment was warm but the windows crackled – it was cold outside.

Yes, he had to think very carefully. But the only thing that kept popping into his head was the phrase, the concept – poor Nettie. But what was 'poor' about her now? She was doing better than she had ever done. She had recovered from modeling, from bigness, and from isolation, and a rich man was showering her with costly gifts.

So what was the source of this threat?

The truth was, he was growing uncomfortable with that 'threatened' hypothesis. The man seemed to be an eccentric, wealthy lush. Hell, they made the world go round.

A physical threat? Not that. Nettie could take care of herself.

What other kinds of threats were there? Spiritual? Psychological? Perhaps. Nettie had been teetering on the edge of something terrible for a while now.

She was owed her periodic breakdowns and he was there to see that she had them in peace.

She had struck him last night. A bad sign. Rufe had never associated that woman with any act of violence – no way, no time. The threat was darker than all that, though.

Freak Town. Freak Town. Rufe remembered his phrase, the one that elicited the assault. He had no idea where he had picked up that phrase.

He started doodling on the table, as if he were in his office. But he had no writing instrument in his hand and there was no yellow pad on the table.

He burst out laughing. Choke on your faggot dreams. Yeah. That is what she had said. Not a bad line.

A wave of bleak nausea assailed the dark little man. So fierce and so sudden that he lay his face down on the table. Was that it? Was she right? Was this all about a dream crashing to earth? But maybe it wasn't the same dream she meant. His dream was simple: that there could be a deep, loving, eternal friendship that could never oh never be torn asunder, a trust that could never be breached.

Nettie was that. Wasn't she? That she was a poor little colored girl come in from the boondocks with a style and a face and a body – that made it more potent. Little Rufe saves Big Nettie. Dark ugly wind whips up lovely Bo Peep and wraps her in the protective embrace of the vortex – keeps the little shepherdess for his own, so no one can ever harm her, so no one can ever get to her.

Was that it? This Albert character had simply stolen her away, and he couldn't bear it. So he had to erect a threat in order to justify intervening, to get her back . . . so that always, in every bar, she was at his side, following his lead, following his advice, admiring him, her hand lightly on his neck, as was her wont.

He went into the kitchen, poured a little milk into a cup, then a shotglass full of bad blackberry brandy. He swallowed his hangover medicine.

There was indeed a beast among them. Snapping. The beast in the jungle. The day Nettie had cut up all her clothes, she was incoherent, obviously half mad. She talked about a beast. He had meant to bring that up again someday, when that insane episode was long in the past. Obviously the beast had been routed, he thought, or slunk back into his lair. If he tries to get my Nettie, I'll beat him back in there again. No use running from that mother fucker. It's you or him.

He washed the cup out. He realized he was sweating. He walked to the mirror and stared at his face. Sweat circled his hairline like a halo.

After showering he lay back down on the bed and put the pillow over his face. I am becoming a jive-ass nigger, he thought, literally squirming on the bedcovers.

Nettie had dreams of her own to choke on – all kinds of dreams.

It doesn't matter what Nettie feels.

It doesn't matter what dreams haunt Uncle Pleasant.

It doesn't matter how sweet-seeming Albert is.

Don't matter. Don't matter. Don't matter.

Is she in trouble?

Yes, yes, yes. It's there. In front of everyone. Shapeless. But coming hard and fast.

Does Little Rufe have the balls to act? What kind of pussy has Little Rufe become . . . high-flying, achieving executive that he is . . . swift, cool, martini-slurping *flâneur* that he is . . . trenchant chronicler of the Big Apple's vagaries that he is . . . self-transformer that he be.

Does Aunt Rufe have the balls?

Lying there, he thought of that old army saying:

—If you don't know where the enemy is, then you don't know what he's doing.

There was another one: Jodie's got your gal and gone.

V.

She was on the horns . . . sitting on the horns of mood. There was sadness at what had happened between her and Rufe. But there was also happiness, because she was anticipating Albert's imminent return from Boston. The dichotomy made her jittery and unfocused. She could not work on her bags or hats and she could not concentrate sufficiently to sketch any new designs.

She prowled the loft until 1 P.M. and then switched on the Fashion Europe Channel, a newly added feature to her cable TV service.

In the afternoon they showed an hour's worth of fast-paced three-minute fashion videos, each one featuring a French, Italian, Japanese, or British designer. There was no commentary, only endless flashy shots with pounding music soundtracks. They ran video excerpts of the runway shows of the various designers, one model after the other, moving lazily, moving quickly, turning, preening, pouting, unbuttoning, teasing, then heading back toward the curtain. When one model was halfway back, another model would appear, moving, strutting, jacket on, jacket off. Sometimes as many as three models at one time on view.

Nettie settled onto the sofa to watch, feeling vaguely uncomfortable. She tried to avoid these programs, but always she seemed to know precisely what hour the shows aired, and before she knew it she was there on the couch, watching.

It wasn't a longing to return to the past, nor a sense of what might have been. After all, she had never made it to the international runway. Before the weight gain, she had done some print ads, some showroom work in the garment center, and some shows put on by high-end suburban restaurants to attract the lunching ladies' crowd.

Watching, there was no bitterness, and no tears. In spite of her reluctance to watch, the images always elicited elation. This made her feel a bit guilty because she had never truly been able to understand her almost pathological desire when younger and thinner to model on the runway. She knew it was the thing itself she craved − not the accompanying glamour and money, although that would have been appreciated. It was the walk she craved. The walk and the look. Remote. Unobtainable.

The first video was of an Italian designer − Marinaro . . . Marinello . . . something like that. She couldn't catch the name. It flashed on and off the screen too quickly. The third model to stride onto the landscape was Naomi Campbell − that singular panther. And then Helena Christensen, with the legs. And Kate Moss. And then a Kenyan girl, a brand new discovery. Without taking any particular effort, Nettie knew the names of most of the super-models. Subliminal.

The next video featured the work of a young French designer. Greens and oranges and lavender, the occasional poppy. A metaphor for the Parisian summer. Skirts that ended just below the buttocks, and billowy tops fastened loosely with string or not at all. The theme running through the day's shows was, apparently, exposed breasts. Some of the girls were showing one breast as the gossamer tops flounced around their upper bodies; others emerged topless, their fingers laced at their chests.

She found herself becoming morose. She watched the screen, almost hypnotized, thinking of Rufe to the exclusion of Albert. She kept staring at the screen, but the only things that registered were the colors.

What had been Rufe's rap about models? In their new iconic roles? She remembered: He had described the world of high fashion at various times as either the revenge of the gay man, a roster of pricey whores in a brothel, a slave auction, or a zoo where you can see birds of paradise strutting about to music.

Nettie folded her arms tightly. She would miss that little man, for all his lunacy. He had said something else, she remembered—A man would have to be crazy to want to fuck one of those preying mantises. It would be like sucking on a wishbone coated with strychnine.

But he had quickly apologized, saying he was not including Nettie or Naomi in that equation. And, he added, if he were straight he'd gladly have either of them and thank his lucky stars for the opportunity. And then he had admitted his preference for Naomi over her, because, he said, he had never liked country girls.

Nettie flipped the set off, pulled her feet up onto the sofa, and stretched out. The country girl comment used to make her mad. She had no idea why Rufe persisted in teasing her that way. She was born in the city. Not a big city, but a city nevertheless: Bruxton. A hundred miles southwest of Chicago. An old industrial city, half black, half white ethnic, and never the twain did meet. All poor, except for a hundred or so WASP families high up on the hill.

She closed her eyes and tried to conjure up Bruxton, the streets, the school, the stores, her mother. But all she saw was Louisa. She could see her friend lurching along in the pair of heels she had taken from beneath Nettie's bed, taken without asking. The two of them were headed to the White Castle one late summer evening and Nettie looked down to see her own new shoes on Louisa's misshapen feet. Louisa never could walk straight.

She glanced at the clock. Two P.M. Albert would

be back in the hotel by five. She ached to see him now. She sat up suddenly and swung her legs over the side. Rufe will come around sooner or later, she thought. He'd forgive her. There would be, as he put it, peace in the realm. All of them lying down together, fangs and claws sheathed. The lions and the lambs.

Part 6

WXY.

When she entered the hotel room he was standing by the closet fully dressed. She started toward him. He halted her with a gesture of his hand.

—What's the matter, Albert? Are you ill?

—No, no. Please, just stand there for a minute, Nettie. Let me look at you. You were all I was thinking about in Boston. Nettie, Nettie, Nettie. I couldn't sleep or work. You kept on drifting in and out of my head. I can't believe it – that we're here together. I have this fear, Nettie, and can't seem to drink it away. I keep thinking I'm going to die and never see you again.

—Don't say that, Albert. Nothing is going to happen to you. Or to me. We are going to be together. No one is going to die.

He rushed over to her and took her hands and kissed them again and again, front and back.

Then he said,—Sit on the bed, Nettie. I want to give you something. I know you don't want any more gifts, but I saw it in Boston and I had to get it. Sit, Nettie, sit.

Shaking her head, half frowning, half smiling at

the futility of forbidding him to buy her things, she sat down on the bed.

This time it was a gift-wrapped box, large. He laid it on the carpet and unpacked the garment. Then he held it up for her to see, against his own body.

She felt that little rush. The rush one gets at the first sight of a piece of clothing one was destined to wear, something meant for oneself.

This certainly was.

It had a designer label, but it was a simple camisole. So beautifully plain that one could mistake the subtly patterned ivory fabric for a washed-out potato sack — if one did not look too closely.

Delicate shoulder straps completed it. She knew it would fit. This only added to her excitement. Large women could rarely find such garments. They were usually made for sylphs. But she had found one. Albert had found it for her. He knew. He handed her the garment.

—Would you put it on for me, Nettie? Could I see what you look like in it?

She stepped out of her shoes and undressed quickly. She slipped the camisole over her head.

—Lord, Albert. It feels like nothing on my skin. Like bath water.

—Wait there, Nettie. Wait there. Just like that.

He went to the other side of the bed and pulled a carton out from under it. This one was long and narrow. He placed it on the bed and pulled out ten, twenty, maybe twenty-five long-stemmed yellow flowers with ferns. Lilies? Orchids? She didn't know.

He thrust all of them into her arms.—From Chile, Nettie. Or Mozambique. Or Sri Lanka, he said.—They come from one of those places.

She cradled the flowers like a child at a wedding. She moved about the room in her camisole, slowly, as if there were musical accompaniment – perhaps a pavane.

Albert slid to the carpet and watched her move. He looked like a frightened, small, sandy-haired boy.

She started toward him, to thank him for all this beauty.

Again he stopped her with a gesture.—Keep moving, Nettie. Please. Keep moving. You look so beautiful, so regal, so perfectly formed. I have never seen anyone walk like you.

She smiled and blew him a kiss, pirouetting in slow motion. Then she began to lower herself onto him.

He went rigid then, and cried out. Called her name. Nettie froze.

—What is it?

—Keep moving, Nettie! he said.—No, wait! Don't do anything. Don't do anything else. I—you'd better go now.

—What are you talking about, Albert? Get up. Get up and come to bed with me.

—No! You must go.

—Go where?

—Leave here. Now. Don't stay. I'll come to you later. Or call. But you must leave now.

She sat down heavily on the bed, light-headed from the scent of the flowers.—Oh, Albert.

—You have to, Nettie. Quickly. I'll explain later.

She began to dress.

He crawled toward her. She saw shame in his face. And love, for her, deep corrosive love.

Rufe sat at a front window table in the small café across the street from the Soho Granada.

It was 7:30 in the evening. A light snow had begun to fall. He had a cappuccino and a fruit tart in front of him. He kept leaning over the table, staring out onto West Broadway, tense, agitated, making little tings with a spoon on the handle of his cup. The chill from the outside, through the glass, was intense.

The café was empty for all practical purposes. Just Rufe and the distracted-looking woman two tables away.

On the seat next to him was a soft black leather carrying case with both handles and a shoulder strap. Rufe rarely carried anything, even when he met clients in an official capacity. And in fact the case on the seat was empty, except for a small pad, two mechanical pencils, seven packets of Bayer aspirin, and a .25 caliber Swiss-made derringer with three rounds in the chamber.

The weapon had been given to Rufe six years ago, by a now-deceased acquaintance. Rufe had never used it and never even handled it before.

Was he going to use it now? Was he going to blow Albert Press to kingdom come?

Rufe didn't know. He didn't know why he had taken the weapon with him. He didn't know what he was going to do about Albert, but he had to do something. He had to confront him somehow. He had to defuse the threat to Nettie . . . he had to make that freak understand Nettie had friends who loved her and were watching out for her, even if their motives were also suspect.

He took out his handkerchief, the beautiful handkerchief in his breast pocket, and wiped the moisture from his lips. I must look like Louis Armstrong near the end, he thought unhappily.

He noticed that the waiter was beginning to look at him with suspicion. It would be best, Rufe reasoned, to sample what he had ordered. He sipped the cappuccino and forked a tiny piece of tart. Both tasted terrible.

Nettie came out of the hotel at 7:45 carrying a large box. The sight of her almost shattered him. He wanted to run across the street and kiss her hands and beg forgiveness for his vulgarity. He wanted her back, any way she wanted to be back.

He recovered quickly. That box, he realized, must contain another gift. What else could it be?

A doorman whistled up a cab for her. She

climbed in and was gone. Now Rufe faced a dilemma. Should he wait for the man to exit the hotel? Or should he go into the hotel to find him? Both options were chancy. The man might not come out. And he, Rufe, might not be able to get in.

Either way, he had to decide on a mode of action. What precisely was he going to say to the man when he confronted him? Was the point just to warn Albert Press to stay away from Nettie? And how was he going to enforce it? Or was the point to find out once and for all whether a real threat existed and what it was?

Too many questions. He was losing his resolve.

But then Press came out of the hotel, not more than ten minutes after Nettie's departure. He wasn't wearing an overcoat or a hat. He stood in the falling snow like an acolyte. Rufe watched him closely. Would he get a cab? If so, Rufe's mission was aborted. Would he go back into the hotel? Would he go to the hotel bar? Rufe grasped his bag and stood up. The waiter brought his check and Rufe paid. He tipped absolutely nothing.

The little black man looked rather like a malevolent pixie. Or an aboriginal in one of Press's more arcane guide books. From a tribe deep in the Amazon rain forest. Except his people weren't head hunters; they were a secret think tank.

He had Karen's table. The one she'd sat at each

time she'd come here to lay in wait for Albert. She went on refusing to leave messages for him at the hotel. That wasn't the way she wanted to do it. Simply walk up to him on the street – say his name – that was the only way.

Each time she waited in the café – sometimes for hours dawdling over coffee or hot chocolate or wine, other times remaining only ten minutes – she swore she would not return. At the end of her vigil she would flee the café and jump into the first taxi she saw. Once back at the hotel, she would pace frenetically, cursing herself for her insane behavior. Then she would take down the suitcase and begin to pack. But before the night was over she found herself phoning the Granada. One more time.

—Mr. Press doesn't answer.

The mystery had doubled in on itself now. It wasn't just a matter of finding out why he had taken up residence at the Granada. It was a matter of why he was so seldom in his room. What was he doing? Was he in a drunk tank? Was he dead?

She pulled the new brown sweater tighter around her shoulders. Even in America, the French were niggardly with heat. What was the pang in her stomach now? The same indecision and tension, or simple hunger? The food in the café did not look very good, but she thought perhaps she ought to order something. She had not been eating right.

It was at the moment she decided to ask the dapper little black man, deep in his own thoughts, if she might have a cigarette from the open pack on his table that she saw Albert.

She must have missed him earlier. Turned her head at precisely the wrong moment. Or perhaps she had been in the ladies' room. No way to tell. But now he was coming out of the hotel, not going in.

He stood at the curb for a long time but he didn't appear to be waiting for a cab. Dressed in a finely checked sports jacket and dark pants. He wore no overcoat. The same wild mane of hair. But he looked so small. She had no memory of his being shorter than she. Wasn't that odd?

Karen watched him, fastened to her chair, while he turned his face up to the falling snow. As if he were drinking it. Every few seconds his knees buckled a little. But then he would right himself.

He must be drunk, she thought.

A drunken dancing bear, she thought. A happy madman. Whatever ridiculous errand he was on, living in that $400-a-night monstrosity, it must be working out well for him.

There was still time to run across the street and confront him. But she did not move.

One of the doormen spoke to him, but Albert waved him away. He was rubbing his hands together now, looking to the left and then to the right.

Karen actually rose from her seat, but only for a second. The blow on her heart knocked her back down. She had never been so tired in her life.

Nothing was going according to plan. She was supposed to fly across the street and pronounce his name softly. And he was supposed to cradle her in his arms and call her by her name. Karen. Not Karen dear or Dear Karen or any variation on that theme. But she did not want Albert Press's arms around her anymore. She no longer wanted to gaze into his ghostly brown eyes or hear him discourse on the wonders of the Prado or list the five points guaranteed to convince any boss to give you a raise.

Albert Press was a clown on his last legs. Swaying with the wind. Karen loathed him. And suddenly she knew that she had been stalking him in order to kill him. That is, to kill what was left of him in herself. If she was to go on living, she had to obliterate him. It was him or her.

She picked up the oversize red napkin and began to weep silently into it, holding back the howl of unbelievable grief in her chest. She felt it all leaving her body now. Like a breaking fever. The love along with the hate and the dammed-up resentment and shame over her self-abasement.

When she looked out again, Albert was gone. And so was the oddly compelling little black man.

Albert Press started to move, not back into the hotel and not into a cab. He walked north on West Broadway at a fast clip.

Rufe walked out and followed, keeping across the street from him and about twenty yards behind.

Albert walked with his head up, his arms swinging easily.

A stroll in the snow, Rufe thought. The freak is strolling. Rufe wrapped his muffler around his face to keep the wind off. His fingers were freezing, so he slung the black case over his shoulder.

At Houston, Albert turned east, crossing not ten yards from where Rufe had paused.

The stroll continued until Albert slipped into a bar near Mott Street.

Rufe waited five minutes outside, and then followed him in. It was a narrow, crowded bar. Albert was near the front, drinking his drink standing up. There were no empty stools. Rufe walked to the end of the bar and ordered a martini.

The noise level inside the bar was almost intolerable. But Rufe stayed detached and kept his eyes glued to the prey. Albert looked different from the time Rufe had seen him in his office. Well, of course the bandage was gone now. But it wasn't just that. He appeared larger, handsomer. Like a man in love. A man getting plenty of pussy – after a fashion, that is. Rufe had a sudden wicked fantasy of just putting his drink down and walking out of the noisy bar, shooting Mr. Press in the back as he exited. Quick. Clean. Never looking back.

Rufe downed his martini as if it were a shot of rye whiskey. He kept his eyes focused on Albert. Something was happening to that sandy-haired man now. He had lowered his head and was rubbing his brow with the glass. Fatigue? Headache? Despair?

Press walked quickly out of the bar, catching Rufe off guard. By the time Rufe got out, Albert was not in sight. Which way? Rufe tried to cross Houston; the cars drove him back. The snow had stopped. Rufe ran to the corner of the Bowery. He caught a glimpse of him. Albert was on the north side of Houston, and walking east. Rufe crossed over at Avenue A and stayed closer this time. He was sweating inside his clothes, and starting to shiver. The thought came to him that he might well die this night, and he didn't give a fuck.

After crossing Avenue C, still on Houston, Albert Press suddenly stepped off the curb and rushed across a narrow strip of roadway onto one of the small concrete islands. He sat down on a stone bench.

What the hell is he doing there, Rufe thought. Is the man a complete lunatic? Only derelicts and junkies sit on these benches. But even they couldn't hack a winter night like this one.

Rufe pressed against the building line and kept vigil. The notion of a sophisticate shivering to death on Houston Street in pursuit of a freak had its ironies, to say the least. Rufe began to sing quietly: 'Miss Otis Regrets.'

A woman passed him . . . stared . . . stopped.— Want something sweet, baby? she mumbled.

Rufe recoiled. The woman was one of the nastiest

black street whores he had ever seen in New York. She wore a blue sweatshirt and green sweatpants covered with scum that looked as if it might be vomit. Her hair was thick, filthy, and matted. Her face was pocked and she had those telltale junkie eyes. Only her smile was within a sane world, but it was not enough.

She spat at him for his refusal, and walked on.

But she walked only a few steps, stared across the road to the island, and started to yell, as if she had located one of her pushers. Yet there was no one on the island but Albert Press.

Rufe watched in horror as Albert crossed back to the sidewalk and embraced the woman and, arm in arm, they vanished into a doorway.

—This place, Simon noted,—is not vintage Rufus.

They were seated in a Greek luncheonette a block from the Manhattan ramp to the Fifty-ninth Street Bridge.

—I eviscerate people who call me Rufus, Rufe said, smiling, fiddling with a water glass. Each one had a cup of coffee in front of him. Simon had a dish of rice pudding as well.

—So, what's the rush? What the hell is going on?

—I need a favor.

—There's nothing I can do for you, Rufe. Or anyone else, for that matter.

—Save the world-weary shit, Rufe replied. He took an envelope out of his jacket pocket and drew five hundred–dollar bills out of the envelope, halfway. Then he laid the package on the table between them.

—Do you see this, Simon?

—Vaguely.

—Three of the bills are for you. Not much for a world traveler like you. But it's tax free. And you don't have to draw any brown pelicans for it.

—And the other two bills?

—I want you to turn a trick with an ugly black whore on Houston Street.

—Dream on.

Rufe picked up one of the hundreds.—This one you give her to take off her clothes for you. You don't have to touch her, much less fuck her. You want her just to talk filthy to you for twenty minutes. She'll think you're really weird. She'll be happy. It'll be the easiest hundred bucks she ever made. She'll love you, Simone.

—How enthralling.

Rufe flicked another hundred.—After this interlude, Simon, it goes without saying that you will act as if you got off on it. Then you offer her another hundred to tell you everything she knows about one of her johns. His name is Albert. There is a description of him in the envelope.

—And who is he?

—That you don't have to know.

—Why don't you do it?

—A white man would be more alluring.

—Oh, right. Junkie whores have very strict racial preferences. What else don't I have to know?

—Will you do it?

—We're not friends anymore, Rufe. You went your way, I went mine. The only thing that connects us is that both ways are shit.

—You know, Simone, sometimes you have a way with words. Did you ever think of a career in hip-hop?

—How important is this to you?

Rufe took a deep drink of the coffee, almost sucking it up, then leaned back in the booth and smiled.

—I'm sitting in a sad railroad station, in Wilmington, Delaware. It's three o'clock in the morning. The air conditioning is busted. The train to New York is late. The bar is shut. I doze. I look up. There's a black boy seated next to me. Maybe eighteen, maybe younger. A farm boy maybe. He's going to New York. He tells me he has no one. Oh, he's a beautiful young man, Simone. Bone hard. Chiseled black face. We talk some more. Music, he's into music. He asks me if I know the big city. He asks me if he can ride along with me on the choo-choo train and will I show him the city when we get there. He asks me if I can give him a place to sleep for a few nights. Yes. Yes. Yes. He exhales and relaxes. His shirt is open. I can see his stomach – ribbed, muscular, lean, an improperly healed scar right over the belly button. It's three o'clock in the morning, Simone. The top button of his jeans is open. He takes my ugly hand. And we just sit there – waiting for the train, in the Wilmington station. Or was it Scranton?

—I don't have the slightest idea what you're talking about.

—Yes or no?

—Yes. Simon picked up the envelope.—But don't call me again, Rufe. From now on, to me, you're a hustler bar on West Tenth Street.

Nettie flicked on the fashion channel. But before she could settle in, she heard the sounds of what seemed to be an altercation in the hallway.

She left the sofa, opened the apartment door and peered out.

The old woman who lived in the rear apartment was screaming in Chinese at a fat black workman wearing strapped denim coveralls over a thick wool sweater. The workman carried a plumber's snake in one hand and a metal attaché case in the other.

Nettie motioned to him. Confused, he walked toward her about ten feet, and stopped.

—She won't let you in, Nettie said.—She won't let anyone in unless her daughter's with them.

—The lady's toilet is backed up. Nobody told me anything about a daughter.

—She works about two blocks from here, Nettie added.

The man looked back at the Chinese woman. Then turned back to Nettie.—She speak English?

—No.

—Could I use your phone for a minute? I better call the office.

Nettie opened the door wider and he walked inside. She pointed to the phone. Then she sat down on the sofa and resumed her fashion TV viewing. She did not listen to the call. A minute later she heard the man say 'Thanks.'

She looked at the workman. Fifty-five to sixty, he was. He stood there watching the screen, his equipment beside him on the floor. He looked oddly familiar to her.

—Pretty girls, he said, pointing to the models on the screen.

—Yes, she agreed.

—Never had a pretty girl like that.

He said the words in a whimsical manner, tinged with ruefulness.

She did not know why, but Nettie was all at once infuriated. And then she realized where she had seen this man before. Back home in Bruxton. Of course, not really him but his legion of brothers. Lounging, laughing, smoking, drinking, calling out to the young girls passing, pooling their money to buy whores and wine, anything for a taste. He was the man who bought Louisa's ass with sweet and sour chicken. When they catcalled Louisa, she was always ready with a sassy, flirtatious answer that made

the men laugh. But when one of them proposi-
tioned Nettie, who only stared sullenly in return, it
was as if she were the one who had done something
offensive. The old lech would turn his anger on
her, his flirtatious banter would descend to vile
cussing, and she would end up running to escape
him. His laughter following as she fled.

Now she was again facing one of them, after all
these years.

She was staring openly at the man.

—So you like them pretty? she asked.

—Oh yeah.

And now the roles were reversed. She was strong.
He was weak. She was the one doing the sizing up.
And she was the one doing the laughing. She was
worshiped by a man worth a thousand of him. The
fury and triumph seemed to bubble out of her.

—Is this pretty? she asked through her teeth. And
then she opened her robe.

She was naked underneath.

—Hey! What you doing?

—Look! Look! I'm asking you. Isn't this pretty?
I'm not one of the pretty girls you never had? Well,
fuck you. I've got a man who could buy and sell
you.

—You crazy, girl, he said. Frightened now, he
picked up his case and headed for the door.

Nettie kept after him, taunting:—I'll tell you why
you never had a pretty woman. You're too fat. And
too ugly. And now you're too old. The only way

you ever got it was to pay for it. I've got a man who could buy and sell you, motherfucker.

The black man stopped. He seemed to be transforming himself. He seemed to be springing up from the ground in a different pattern. He dropped his tools and with an inarticulate cry rushed her – knocking her back onto the sofa with his elbow. She began to flail her arms on the man's back.

Whatever was happening . . . the violence . . . quickly became something else.

He turned her over and pulled the bathrobe up. He climbed on her from the back.

His cock was large. She was dry. Flint scraping rock. He screamed out curses as he pushed. And then he was all the way in and pumping. His body was crushing her.

She felt stabs of pain and then inchoate pleasure, depending on the rise and fall of his body. The sofa fabric was cutting off her air.

Yes, Albert could buy and sell just about anybody, but he would not take her for free. The way she wanted him to. She began to call out his name and then she let out a strange, loving moan that drove the man on her into a frenzy.

Nettie heard a terrible scream close to her ear and a second later the weight was off her body. Gasping for air, she sat up.

The man was on the floor, his penis dangling out

of his underpants, pathetically soft now. His coveralls way down around his ankles. His belly huge and fig-colored.

The fat old man was writhing in pain, arching his back against the floor, grasping and pounding at his thighs. It was obvious he had severe cramps in both.

Nettie pushed up silently from the sofa. She knotted her bathrobe tightly around herself and walked directly to the sewing table.

The man's cries were becoming softer and softer as the cramping receded. She did not move to help him. She felt no compassion for him, and no hatred.

—What next? she said aloud.—Jesus, what next? Could anything else possibly happen? No. Not possible. Now everything had happened. All the permutations.

Nettie looked down at the workman and saw horror in his face. He was staring at her right hand. There was a pair of six-inch shears in her fist.

She let out a gasp and dropped them heavily into the sewing box.

The old man scrambled to his feet and nearly tore the apartment door from its hinges.

She stood where she was for a long time, but finally crossed the room. Then she slid the door closed behind him.

—Excellent, excellent, Rufe told the post-punk girl

bartender as he sipped the martini she had made for him.

Rufe was just being polite. In fact the drink was horrendous. He didn't expect a good martini here. After all, the place he had selected to meet Simon in after the mission was a white druggie hang-out on Avenue A, hardly martini country.

Rufe had been in this place only a couple of times before. The human wreckage was everywhere. It was fascinating to watch them as they sat huddled over their drinks staring at God knows what in their heads.

The jukebox, anyway, was without parallel – a Joe Tex extravaganza. And the complete works of Gene Chandler. And the complete works of Gene Pitney. Not to mention folk music, which Rufe always found charming, like finding an old invitation at the bottom of a drawer.

In fact, he avoided the bar simply out of the fact of his graciousness. He knew his presence unnerved people like these. Besides, it was not a place he could take Nettie; she would be appalled. That was Nettie's only flaw over time as a bar companion – she did not appreciate the necessity for diversity.

Two bad martinis, the entire *Blond on Blond* album, and then Simon walked in. It was almost ten o'clock. He was wearing a suit and tie for the mission, which Rufe found appropriate. He looks rather like the young George Harrison, Rufe thought, absurdly.

Simon sat down next to Rufe and ordered a tonic water with lime.

—I can't hang around long, Rufe, he said.

—No need.

—I found her. I did exactly as you said. The hundred-dollar bills made her eyes pop out.

Rufe was about to ask what particular brand of trash she had talked. But then he realized Simon had been crying; he could see the puffiness under his eyes. So what he said was simply—Did she remember that man?

—Yes. He's a good and regular customer. She finds him on Houston Street once or twice a week. He pays well.

—And?

—It's very simple. It's not what you think.

Rufe waited. Simon lowered his voice a bit:— Always the same. Always the same, if you can believe her. Look, Rufe, she's in the last stage of decomposition, for godsake.

—I am bearing that in mind.

Okay. She has a room a bit larger than your bathroom. She doesn't take off her clothes. He doesn't take off his clothes. He lays down on the floor. She squats down over him and urinates on his forehead.

—What?

—You deaf, man? You heard me. Pisses in his face. Maybe the clown thinks he's being anointed.

Rufe felt the strength ebbing out of his body,

Samson with a haircut. He had trouble maintaining himself on the stool.

—Rufe, what the fuck is this about?

—About?

—Yes. What's going on?

—What this is about, boy, you would not understand.

—Stop that patronizing shit. What won't I understand?

—Degradation.

Simon's burst of laughter was almost hysterical.— I wouldn't understand degradation? You have a short memory, don't you?

—My memory's just fine, miss. You think you know what degradation even means? Just because some of the cadavers at Jimmy's made you put out? Because you once fucked for your supper?

The bar had gone absolutely silent except for Rufe's storming voice.

—You'd better shut your filthy mouth, Rufe.

—You think you got any idea in this sick, whoring world what it means to be degraded? Fuck degraded. Owned. Rufe was standing up on his toes now, screaming into Simon's face.

—Oh, I get it now, it's a black thing, right? You have the nerve to play a race card on me . . . me!

—Yeah, you. Why not you? You think you understand about being a nigger 'cause those motherfuckers used you? Or 'cause you keep up your pretty tan so nice? Who thinks you're a nigger, Simon? Who ever treated you like a nigger?

Simon's face wrinkled horribly. It took him a long time to speak.—Okay. I'm off, Rufe.

—You got that right, you pitiful cucaracha. Go have your breakdown somewhere else.

Simon blinked and swallowed hard. Then he placed his hand for a moment, only a brief moment, on Rufe's shoulder.—Did I ever thank you right, Rufe? For looking out for me the way you did?

After a minute, Rufe nodded.

When Simon was gone, Rufe took his seat again, waiting to recover some of his strength. The rage within him waxed and waned, waxed and waned.

He ordered straight vodka. He needed to be clear-headed now. Yes, it was all becoming clear as vodka.

Albert Press was turning Nettie into an insect. The Termite Queen.

A devout courtier, he licks her all day to keep her sexually intense.

She is exalted like the lord of hosts, only to be turned into a slave for the hive. The hive needs her eggs.

Rufe understood. Press was destroying Nettie, tightening the shackles.

The man knew what he was doing and he paid penance for it with a urinating whore.

Rufe pulled the black case onto his lap. Reached inside and ran his palm lightly over the derringer.

Then he closed his eyes and breathed deeply. His strength was coming back. But he had miles to go.

Part 7

Z.

Prego stared thoughtfully at the table on which lay the corpse of a white man. While staring, he played with a business card which had been found in the dead man's wallet. It was his own.

Prego was by the corpse's midsection and staring toward the head. Behind the head stood Loache, a detective from Manhattan South. And next to him stood a small Asian, the assistant medical examiner.

Even though the man's face was a mess, the ID was easy for Prego because of the almost-healed mayhem on the right side of the face, and the thick sandy hair. It was Albert Press.

The assistant ME moved the table just a bit and said:—He was shot twice in the face at close range, one of the bullets entering his left eye. The weapon was probably a .22 or .25 caliber handgun. Ballistics is checking the one slug recovered. He has an old but bad slash wound on his right cheekbone. The stitches were removed long before the shooting.

—You say he was staying at a Soho hotel? Prego asked Loache.

—Yeah. Why?

—The man lived uptown, near Lincoln Center.

—Hotel manager says he had been there for weeks.

—Okay.

—We know a lot more, Loache announced.— He received a phone call in his room at 3 A.M. He left the hotel about fifteen minutes later. The body was found by sanitation workers about 5:30 in the small park at Canal and Sixth, lying face down behind the fence. There's a taxi garage abutting the park. We have one driver who might have seen something. Around three-thirty. A kid and an older man sitting together in the cold on one of the benches. The driver had seen the kid in the area before. Hispanic, wears a Chicago Cubs cap. The way I figure it, it's cut and dried. The kid took the cash, left the credit cards. Horny rich fag in hotel room. Can't sleep. Gets a call from trick. Ashamed to bring the kid up to the hotel. Meets him in park around the corner. But something goes wrong. Before Richie Rich can get to suck cock, the kid tells him prices have gone up. Richie Rich refuses. Trick tussles with him and ends up blowing him to kingdom come. Not pretty. But it'll fly.

Fly is right, thought Prego. He had known all along there was something off about Albert Press – but he would not have figured it was that. Not that at all.

—One thing's weird, noted Loache.—The hotel

manager says the man had a knockout visitor from time to time. A black lady.

—Light skin? Prego asked.

—How'd you know that?

—Just guessed.

—She could've been his drug connection, huh? Or maybe this Press went both ways, Loache said.

Prego didn't want to pursue it any further. It was no longer his case. He thanked them and left.

They were ensconced at the end of the bar in a beautiful new restaurant on the edge of Gramercy Park. The motif was sedately nautical. The cuisine was Iberian seafood. But neither of them was there to eat. Rufe was not standing. He sat erect on the shiny black barstool. Ebony.

Nettie was standing. Standing tall, almost defiant. She looked imposing in her transparent brown top, the camisole visible beneath it. She wore no hat. The breathtaking Indian blanket was draped over her jacket on the empty barstool next to her. It kept her warm, she found, no matter how low the temperature fell. Albert had been dead a week.

Nettie was drinking bourbon. Sometimes she swayed as if to music. But there was no music in the restaurant. She turned outward, her back resting against the bar rail.

—You know, Rufe, I meant what I told you. I loved the man. I doubt if I ever will have feelings like that again for anyone. Something's been ripped out of me. I don't even want to feel anything again.

At those words, Rufe felt a fist close around his heart. He drank water.

She lifted her chin. Brave.—See, he never made love with me. Not in the regular way. He wanted to, but he couldn't. But he did love me. I know it.

He was a succubus, Rufe told himself.

—Why was he in the park that night, Rufe? Why would he go out? If he wanted a drink there was a bar in the hotel. And all kind of liquor in the cold chest, right there in his room. They say he got a lot of phone calls the week before he died. All from a woman. But that night the call was from a man. Some man phoned him in the middle of the night and Albert left the hotel a few minutes later. Who were those people? What did they want with him? They had to be the ones who killed him, right?

Rufe's eyes closed for a minute.

Albert's voice had been thick with sleep when he picked up the phone in his hotel room that night.

—Hello, Mr. Press? Ahoy there. I'm Nettie's friend, the one who passed your gift on to her. We're downtown drinking, Mr. Press, and Nettie wants you to come out and play with us. We'll be waiting for you in the park off Sixth.

Rufe had made the call from the lounge across the avenue. The payphone there was near a window. So he could watch when Albert stumbled into the park. He could see the boy fall into step beside Albert.

—I told you what they said in the newspaper, didn't I? Nettie asked, angry.—That he must have had a secret. He was living some kind of double life. He was in the park because his nature made him go out looking for what he needed and the trick killed him for his money. It's bullshit, Rufe. He wasn't gay. The way he treated me? He couldn't have been.

—No, Rufe said.

The thing is, a freak set like golden showers was nothing new or shocking. If Rufe had heard that any other two people were into that, it wouldn't have fazed him at all. But this had been different. Albert Press acted out all his vilest wishes on a surrogate for Nettie – and while he lavished chaste love and bank-breaking gifts on Nettie, she was his surrogate skanky black whore. One was the other. Of course Press knew better but he could not overcome.

And the horror of it, Rufe had thought as he fell asleep last night, was that Press might have loved her. Take away the confusion, the enfeebling self-loathing, the alcohol, yes always the alcohol, and he might've been left with nothing but love for Nettie. But who was going to take those things away?

—It's like you always tell me, Rufe, when I get crazy and start losing sleep over something stupid.

You always say, There's a simple explanation for everything.

—I'm sorry. What did you say?

—I'm saying Albert was killed for some reason. Maybe the police will never know it and maybe I'll never know it. But there has to be a simple explanation. He came into my life for a reason. And I'm mourning him for a reason. She wiped at her eyes.—Otherwise there's no . . .

She broke off there with a heartbreaking little laugh.—Sorry, Rufe. Oh shit, man, I must be talking out of my head. Mercy!

He rotated on his stool, kindness in his smile.— No need to apologize, darling. In fact I think now is the perfect time to change libations. Strong emotions such as these call for cognac.

End

The violent young men would laugh at the old folks and their follies. Those ten-cents-a-week life insurance scams in particular earned their mirth.

Mr. Eldon Lassiter was Nettie's mother's insurance man and he had been coming around once a week to collect ever since Nettie was a toddler. Mr. Lassiter, who tipped his hat to Nettie's mother. And in the fullest part of the Midwest summer, his sleeveless white shirt sticking to his back. Sometimes a peppermint for Nettie.

That summer when she was going on twelve, she had put her foot down and refused to attend Bible school. When her mother went off to work, she drank the leftover coffee and clapped through the house in her mother's white mules. Soap operas all morning. Interview shows. It began that way. Lassiter had knocked, found her in her green robe and her mother's white mules. A regular little housewife, he said.

Nettie, defying the first rule of life as her mother had laid it down, took to leaving the front door unlocked.

Nettie's room was at the back. She was lying on her blue sheets, fiddling with herself. Mr. Lassiter stood in the doorway watching. He never spoke.

He still tipped his hat when Nettie's mother was around. While they talked and exchanged dollars for receipts, Nettie would retreat to her room and softly close the door behind her. When he came around a day or two later, when Nettie's mother was at work, he would ask Nettie to tell him what she had been doing behind the locked door. And after I leave, he asked, at night, what then? She would tell him. After a while he took over from her, duplicating her every movement down to the smallest nuance.

Nettie took care to hide the things he gave her, hide them well – deep inside the closet, or in a separate laundry sack beneath the regular one, or inside her shoe. Anklets. Little, little earrings. A Spanish comb. A linen shift with rosebuds at the squared neckline. It was a woman's dress, but Nettie was tall and it fit her beautifully.

It was a long time before he kissed her on the mouth. She wanted to be kissed on the mouth, like in the movies. And that first time he did it, his finger was inside her. She began to shake uncontrollably, full of fear at what would happen next, but she could see him smiling and so figured: nothing very bad. Something 'good' in fact, because that is what he kept murmuring.—It's good, isn't it? Is that good? Feel good, Nettie?

July.

His trousers off by August. As many kisses on the mouth as she wanted. Nettie in the ice-blue panties and the matching teddy he so loved lifting over her head so that he might kiss her tiny red nipples. He had not entered her yet. But she was holding him tightly down there, following the bloom of his erection from first bud to emission.

They had forgotten, that one afternoon, to lock up behind him. She had met him naked at the door and he had become too excited even to have his coffee. Like always, he was using his finger on her, solicitous, asking if it was good – and she was lost in it, nodding her yesses, agreeing in fact that it was time they made love like real grown-ups, that she was ready for it. Nettie was lifting her hips up slightly, following his directions, and when she turned her head toward the doorway, Louisa was standing there.

One scream came from Louisa and the answering one from Nettie herself. Louisa was on Lassiter suddenly, a pair of shears raised high above her head. The white man fumbled and struggled with her. There was blood on the blue sheet.

Nettie at first wrestled with Louisa, who was much stronger, but then in one movement turned on the white man.—Kill him! she heard herself scream.

Lassiter knocked Louisa over and the scissors went

flying across the room. He was gone within seconds. He did not look back.

The girls decided. They made a solemn pact. They would never tell Louisa's mother that the insurance man had tried to rape Nettie. First off, it would shame Nettie too much. And, too often when those things happened, it was the young girl who was blamed.

**Also by Charlotte Carter and
published by Serpent's Tail**

Rhode Island Red

'This Grace Jones lookalike with a degree in French is a splendid creation' *Sunday Telegraph*

'Jazz addicts have a treat in store with *Rhode Island Red*, a book so filled with affection for the form that Charlie Parker seems almost to be another character . . . It is refreshing to find a heroine who has both a rock-solid moral center and a sense of humor' *Donna Leon*

'*Rhode Island Red* is elegiac and musical—especially if you prefer bebop to hip-hop. Nan is a wonderful character: a dreamer, head in the clouds, feet on the ceiling. Charlotte Carter has managed to be funky and dreamy at the same time' *Liza Cody*

'Welcome to this year's most original fictional detective—a sassy, black intellectual and saxophonist who is plunged into mayhem when an undercover cop gets killed in her apartment. Sharp, funny and beautifully underscored with jazzy prose riffs' *Good Housekeeping*

'Sex and jokes and a love for jazz which blows hot, cool and true from beginning to end' *Literary Review*

Nanette is doing ok playing her saxophone out on the street. Sure, her boyfriend Walter doesn't think it's any way for a black woman with a Masters degree in French to carry on, but she's happy.

Then things start happening. A strange man wants her to explain the mysteries of Charlie Parker. Walter wants to get married. An undercover cop dies in her apartment . . .

Fast, sweet and funny, *Rhode Island Red* is a classic New York thriller, the story of a Spike Lee heroine in a Woody Allen world.

Coq au Vin

'The love affair between jazz, black musicians and Paris is an eternal story; Carter illuminates it with rare intelligence and a gripping vortex of thrills, feeling and wit. An author for the future' *Time Out*

'Carter has an incredibly hot property here: Nanette Hayes may be the most charismatic crime-fiction heroine to appear in the last decade' *Booklist*

'Charlotte Carter has what impresses me more than just about anything in a crime writer: the practised discipline needed to craft functional, human sentences which flow one into the next without embellishment or posturing' *Crime Time*

Nanette, the singular, sax-playing heroine of *Rhode Island Red*, finds herself on a trip back to the land of her dreams. Nan's on a plane to Paris, in search of her wild and wicked Aunt Vivian. But by the time she gets there Vivian's gone, no forwarding address.

So what's a girl to do in Paris in the springtime? Why, fall in love with the first cute young dread-locked autodidact she sets her eyes on, of course. And so Nanette and André embark on a crazy trawl through the jazz-fired world of Paris black expats in search of Aunt Viv and her mysterious one time lover, a legendary bluesman named Little Rube Haskins. Meanwhile a killer is always just one step ahead of them.

Funny, sexy, dangerous and impossibly romantic, *Coq au Vin* is a mystery set amid one of the twentieth century's enduring love affairs—the one between black America and Paris.

Drumsticks

Sharp-witted, sax-playing Nanette Hayes is back on the mean streets of New York. A gift 'mojo doll' from mysterious Harlem folk artist Ida Williams starts turning her luck around real good. When Ida is suddenly shot to death in the middle of Nanette's new uptown gig, things take a turn for the worse and the guilt-stricken saxophonist plunges into Ida's checkered past and, to her surprise, the unsolved murder of a rising rap star.

The rhythms and riffs of the city come ferociously alive in this smart, streetwise New York thriller. Edgy, unpredictable, and always the real deal, *Drumsticks* gives us Nanette Hayes at the top of her freewheeling, irreverent game—and Charlotte Carter at her inventive, ever-original best.